The Evildoers

David Adjmi

A SAMUEL FRENCH ACTING EDITION

SAMUEL
FRENCH

FOUNDED 1830

SAMUELFRENCH.COM
SAMUELFRENCH-LONDON.CO.UK

FOR PRODUCTION ENQUIRIES

UNITED STATES AND CANADA
Info@SamuelFrench.com
1-866-598-8449

UNITED KINGDOM AND EUROPE
Plays@SamuelFrench-London.co.uk
020-7255-4302

Each title is subject to availability from Samuel French, depending upon country of performance. Please be aware that *THE EVILDOERS* may not be licensed by Samuel French in your territory. Professional and amateur producers should contact the nearest Samuel French office or licensing partner to verify availability.

MUSIC USE NOTE

Licensees are solely responsible for obtaining formal written permission from copyright owners to use copyrighted music in the performance of this play and are strongly cautioned to do so. If no such permission is obtained by the licensee, then the licensee must use only original music that the licensee owns and controls. Licensees are solely responsible and liable for all music clearances and shall indemnify the copyright owners of the play(s) and their licensing agent, Samuel French, against any costs, expenses, losses and liabilities arising from the use of music by licensees. Please contact the appropriate music licensing authority in your territory for the rights to any incidental music.

IMPORTANT BILLING AND CREDIT REQUIREMENTS

If you have obtained performance rights to this title, please refer to your licensing agreement for important billing and credit requirements.

THE EVILDOERS was developed in part by the Sundance Institute Theatre Program in June 2006. It was directed by Rebecca Bayla Taichman. Mame Hunt was the dramaturg. The cast was as follows:

JERRY . . . . Geoffrey Nauffts

CAROL . . . . Johanna Day

MARTIN . . . . Michael Stuhlbarg

JUDY . . . . Carla Harting

THE EVILDOERS premiered at Yale Repertory Theatre (James Bundy, Artistic Director; Victoria Nolan, Managing Director) on January 18, 2008. It was directed by Rebecca Bayla Taichman; set design was by Riccardo Hernandez, costume design was by Susan Hilferty, lighting design was by Stephen Strawbridge, sound design was by Bray Poor; the dramaturg was Michael Walkup. The Production Stage Manager was Joanne E. McInernery. The cast was as follows:

JERRY . . . . Stephen Barker Turner

CAROL . . . . Johanna Day

MARTIN . . . . Matt McGrath

JUDY . . . . Samantha Soule

CHARACTERS

The Thernstroms:

JERRY THERNSTROM: Possesses the old-world affectations and speech of an older WASP-y type, as well as the glow of narcissism and self-containment that is specific to New York psychoanalysts. Habituated to luxury and privilege – to the extent that he just blends in with it. Outwardly polite, slightly eccentric, nerdishly academic and also a little abstracted, out of touch. Has a true goofy, silly side to him and also a quietly pained detachment that – by the end of the play – opens into chaos and self-loathing. Late thirties to early forties; right before the cusp of middle age.

CAROL THERNSTROM: Jerry's wife. A wedding planner who is intensely cynical about marriage. She is quick-witted, fashionable, controlling, meticulous (i.e., *compulsive*), self-conscious, literate, and wears all this like a kind of breastplate, or armor. But deep down she knows something in her is dying, or has died; her conscience is bothering her. The discomfiture comes out as hostility. There's something childlike and untouched in her that no one sees. A woman in her forties who takes care of herself, or a woman in her mid-thirties who is aging prematurely – either way, the lines are showing.

The Goldstroms:

MARTIN GOLDSTROM: Jerry's best friend from boarding school. An anesthesiologist. Has a warmth, a naifish sweetness and desire to learn. *Intensely* emotional, but tries to conceal this with varying degrees of success. Develops a deep, agonizing, insatiable spiritual longing throughout the course of the play, as well as a profound – and finally *pathological* – need to connect to people, to himself, to something authentic and rooted. Jerry's age, maybe a year younger.

JUDY GOLDSTROM: The fragile, under-confident and somewhat neurotic wife of Martin. She *works* to conceal her obsessiveness and neuroses – she's embarrassed by them; will admit to her "inappropriate" frailties out of both politeness and the need to exhibit "self-awareness." Her respect for decorum is a default. Younger than Martin.

SETTING

New York: A haute restaurant, the Thernstroms' Manhattan penthouse, the Goldstroms' colonial home in Westchester

TIME

Autumn, an unspecified present

NOTE ON STYLE

The tone and style of this play both undergo rather tortuous shifts. This is deliberate and in perfect keeping with the play's content. Certain ideas about Christianity and Christian Fundamentalism I borrowed (all right, stole outright) from the extraordinary Slavoj Žižek – particularly his work in *On Belief* and *The Puppet and the Dwarf.*

Also indispensable to the writing of this play was Stanley Cavell's remarkable book on the Hollywood comedy of remarriage entitled *Pursuits of Happiness.*

I am completely indebted to my conversations with my dear friend Geoffrey McDonald – whose devotion to theology and philosophy has been a touchstone and inspiration to me for the past decade. He is everywhere in this play.

The Evildoers uses several works as intertexts: *Strangers on a Train* (both Highsmith and Hitchcock), Ibsen's *The Wild Duck*, Mary Shelley's *Frankenstein*, Carl Dreyer's beautiful and mysterious *Ordet*, and Preston Sturges's *The Lady Eve*, paramount among them.

The Evildoers is in three parts:
    One: Strangers on a Train
    Two: The Fright of Real Tears
    Three: Breaking Up
The play should be performed with an intermission after Act Two, Scene 2, and an additional short break between Acts Two and Three.

NOTE ON TEXT

A double slash (//) indicates either an overlap or a jump – i.e., no break between the end of one character's speech and the beginning of the following speech (thanks Caryl Churchill).

Speech in parentheses indicates either a sidetracked thought – or footnote – within a conversation, or a shift in emphasis with *no* transition.

A [STOP] is a *(Pause)* followed by either a marked shift in tone or tempo (like a cinematic jump-cut or a quantum leap) or *no* change in tempo whatsoever – somewhat like putting a movie on *(Pause)* and then pressing play. These moments in the play are less psychological than energetic. They have a kind of focused yet unpredictable stillness, something akin to martial arts, where there is preparedness in the silence. Where a lunge or a swift kick can be delivered from seemingly out of nowhere: quickly, invisibly. Where the energy can shift dramatically in a nanosecond.

ACKNOWLEDGEMENTS

The writing of this play was made possible with funding from the Helen Merrill Foundation, the Jerome Foundation, the Ovid Foundation, and the incredibly generous patronage of Jim McCarthy, Gloria Peterson and family. The play benefited from work at the Sundance Institute Theatre Program. Thanks to Philip Himberg, Mark Subias, Morgan Jenness, Kathy Sova, Stephen Willems, everyone at MCC Theater and the Playwrights Coalition, the Playwrights' Center, Polly Carl, Paul Rusconi, Adam Greenfield, Kip Fagan, Kristen Kosmas, David Brooks, Heidi Schreck, Victoria Stewart, and the preternaturally incisive Bronwen Bitetti. Special thanks to Mame Hunt, Deb Stover and the brilliant quartet of actors with whom I was blessed to work at Sundance: Johanna Day, Carla Harting, Geoffrey Nauffts and Michael Stuhlbarg. The play, particularly the third part, benefited immensely from a workshop at the Royal Court Theatre that would never have happened were it not for the efforts of Dominic Cooke; thanks to him as well as to Lyndsey Turner, Lia Williams, Nancy Crane, Peter Sullivan and Aden Gillett. And to Raul Esparza, Jessica Hecht, Laila Robins and Peter Frechette for their immeasurable contributions to this play in a later workshop. To James Bundy – who walks the walk and whose money is where his mouth is – and to the lovely, devoted, and deeply authentic Jennifer Kiger. And finally an enormous thank you and sigh of relief to the magnificent Rebecca Taichman for her Jesuitical attention to, and belief in, my work.

Never say marriage has more joy than pain.

– Euripides, *Alcestis*

We must all hear the universal call to like your neighbor just like you like to be liked yourself.

– George W. Bush

ACT ONE

1.

(The tail end of **JERRY** *and* **CAROL***'s anniversary dinner.)*

*(***JERRY** *is at the same low-level drunkenness that he'll remain at through most of the play.)*

*(***JUDY** *is wearing* **CAROL***'s ring, her arm extended upward.)*

*(***MARTIN** *is noticeably withdrawn at the opening of the play. The scene begins at a breakneck, rapid-fire speed, lots of overlaps, etc.)*

JUDY. Look you can see your // reflection

JERRY. And you *know* Judy the *stones* actually are // from BURMA

CAROL. *Judy. //*

JERRY. And they have these *caves //*

JUDY. Wait: //

CAROL. No hold it up to the light //

JUDY. *(extending her arm a bit higher)* Wait I think I went to Burma Is // Burma

JERRY. Oh you did //

JUDY. My father, he traveled a lot on business is Burma – ? we went to all // these places

JERRY. Well they //

JUDY. Cambodia Laos //

JERRY. *(pouring drinks for himself and* **CAROL***)* they have these MARvelous caves you see Judy they're just these *treasure* chests these *troves,* you see // they're, they're

9

CAROL. *(refusing* JERRY*'s pour)* (no thank you) //

JERRY. *(continued)* like PIrate ships, FILLed with jewels, *brimming,*

CAROL. *(to* JUDY*)* but it's nice isn't it //

JUDY. My arm hurts //

CAROL. If you hold it up to the light you – are you alright – //you can

JUDY. (I'm fine.)

CAROL. see how the stones are faceted (the cut // I mean:)

JUDY. *(lowering her arm)* I mean my arm hurts but it's OK – did you – ?

CAROL. Look at the *in*set –

JUDY. what did you get Jerry?

JERRY. She got me one of those high-definition *televisions* //

JUDY. Oh //

JERRY. which is just a miracle, I mean the *colors,* the *hues* – those greens, *green* plants – I mean my *god* I've never seen such *green* plants – it's like a tropical rain forest right in my *living* room – I mean when I see a plant on television Judy I feel it photosynthesizing right on my *coffee* table!

JUDY. What brand // is it?

JERRY. And she got me some *terrific* – DVDs

JUDY. Really?

JERRY. *DVDs,* Carl Dreyer, uhhh yes, with a lot of *extras,*

JUDY. "Extras?"

JERRY. Antonioni (actually I'm delivering a paper in Geneva you know // on)

JUDY. *When, oh you are?*

JERRY. It's just a little something, a little something I...

CAROL. He's // always

JERRY. Well it's nothing really it's – just some fluff I scribbled down on a paper napkin...I can't – ha ha – I can't even read my ha-ha my-my own writing.

JUDY. *(smiling politely)* That sounds fun.

CAROL. Why.

JUDY. It just sounds fun.

CAROL. Really, that sounds fun? a bunch of middle-aged *analysts* jerking off over Monica *Vitti*?

JERRY. (Well, it's a bit more than *that* // sweetheart.)

JUDY. Monica Vitti isn't she the one – you know? I'm sorry – can I talk about this?

(beat)

MARTIN. About what?

JUDY. It's OK? I don't know if I'm going off topic.

MARTIN. It's OK honey just speak.

JUDY. OK, so, is Monica Vitti – she's that one with the nuclear waste?

(MARTIN just looks at her.)

MARTIN. The what?

JUDY. That nuclear waste? With the movie, with the nuclear waste?

JERRY. *Red Desert* //

JUDY. And she sticks her hand out – she does

(JUDY imitates Monica Vitti's gesture.)

those – those – *expressive* things with the tendons

(She accidentally spills a glass – MARTIN gets some of it on his lap.)

in her (oh I'm *sorry* – oh let me.)

(She wipes up a bit of spilled soda with a napkin.)

I'm sorry I – are you OK honey? I'm so maladroit! A – haha – I'm so "maladroit" – isn't that funny? Isn't that a funny thing to say. "I'm maladroit"?

(MARTIN says nothing.)

JERRY. Now nobody's *maladroit* Judy, it's just coke Judy, it's perfectly OK.

JUDY. But – you know – three cans of coke can shut down your immune system for a whole day, did you know that?

(She laughs. No one else does.)

MARTIN. And so the idea was, what, you took your engagement ring –

CAROL. Yes

MARTIN. I didn't finish my sentence. *(beat)* So you took it and you decided to //

JERRY. *(drunk)* We took // it!

JUDY. *(regarding the ring)* I love the color; the red? it's like the kind of red your eyes get when you *cry*; do you know what I mean?

CAROL. I don't cry.

JUDY. *(taking it as a joke)* everyone cries Carol.

CAROL. *(polite smile) No*, I'm more what the French call um.

[STOP]

Oh-look-it's *late* Look how late it is Jerry Oh // we need the check.

JERRY. *(sings to himself drunkenly)* "You made me love you...I didn't want to do it"

(Dah dah // dah dah dah...)

MARTIN. Can I speak?

JUDY. Of course you can honey. *(to everyone)* He wants to speak.

(beat)

MARTIN. All right: so explain this to me: so you have this idea: you say "alright: let's take this engagement ring" and you // say

CAROL. Like a protective band –

MARTIN. What?

CAROL. *(retracting)* No nothing, go on.

MARTIN. You say alright: "so" //

JERRY. "Darling:"

MARTIN. "So Jerry – OK – let's add these rubies around the diamond?" //

CAROL. But not rubies they're garnets //

MARTIN. All right // garnets

(**JERRY** *attempts to refresh* **CAROL**'s *drink.*)

CAROL. (No thank you darling) – not that it's really of any significance or anything but basically Jerry and I decided, you know we've been married for however many years, seven,

MARTIN. eight

CAROL. eight, that's right eight years and we just thought //

JERRY. *(munching on a petit four)* Eight! //

CAROL. (And you know I think diachronically not –) well whatever, and we thought, we said uh it'll be nice won't it to add some stones around that thing, that diamond, won't that be nice, because it's just sitting there, and it wants protection //

JERRY. "protection"

CAROL. it's lonely, it wants other stones //

JERRY. *(ebullient)* It's a LONELY STONE!!

CAROL. And we wanted to jazz it up (OK well I hate that phrase but you know what I // mean –)

MARTIN. "Jazz it up"?

CAROL. Not – NO not in a *vulgar* way, but in a (well why, you think it's vulgar?)

MARTIN. It's your ring // Carol.

JUDY. (It's lovely)

CAROL. You think it's vulgar.

(**MARTIN** *looks at her.*)

What?

MARTIN. Well Carol I mean you wouldn't, say, add *arms* to the Venus de Milo would you?

CAROL. No but how do I have access to the Venus defucking Milo? // and what does

MARTIN. Well //

CAROL. it have to do with – why are you being so cryptic // and weird

MARTIN. Well I'm just thinking off the top of // my head –

CAROL. This is such a dumb // conversation

MARTIN. Because that would be – it's not dumb //

CAROL. Yes it is!

JUDY. He's stressed out.

MARTIN. I mean, yes, she's armless, but she's somehow – she's more *lovely* without arms //

JERRY. Who.

MARTIN. Because she's a symbol, she's mutilated but she's symBOLically "whole" and if you added arms to the Venus de Milo it would – it would be like – somehow – cutting off a normal person's arms and mutilating THEM do you see what I mean?

CAROL. *(coyly)* Don't put pants on the piano legs Martin.

MARTIN. I'm not being clear – I know // that –

CAROL. Why don't you just say "I hate your gauche fucking ring" do you think that's going to *shatter* me –

MARTIN. That's not what I'm saying,

CAROL. *What* are you saying?

MARTIN. I'm saying – forget it it's not important –

CAROL. What.

MARTIN. You don't want to hear what I'm saying never mind.

CAROL. No I hear what you're saying you're saying I – I'm "mutilating" my ring because I added *stones* to it? That's just dumb, I don't get it //

MARTIN. Well I guess I'm just dumb.

JERRY. He's not *dumb* // darling.

MARTIN. Well for most people marriage is sacred //

CAROL. "Most people"?

MARTIN. Marriage // – *yes* most people

CAROL. For "most people" a marriage license Martin do you realize has all the stature of a *parking* ticket?

MARTIN. But don't you think that the // *linking of two LIVES*

CAROL *(smiling)* No but do you *realize* that? That it means *nothing*, that nobody gives a *shit*?

(beat)

JUDY. But – you're a wedding planner Carol.

CAROL. So?

MARTIN. So don't // you

CAROL. NO – do YOU find some deep existential meaning in anesthetizing people all day,

MARTIN. It's not // the same

CAROL. And what does a marriage contract *do* Martin, historically, huh, what did it do: do you know?

MARTIN. No Carol WHAT did it do?!

CAROL. It gave two members of the opposite sex *permission* to use each others sexual *organs* for pleasure. And then the woman agrees to give the children the man's name to establish paternity so he can have heirs and she does this in exchange for protection.

MARTIN. You're just crass.

CAROL. But I'm speaking from an historical vantage –

MARTIN. So //

CAROL. but now who even *wants* kids anymore, they're they're just accoutrements or. They're like little tote bags or something, they're like little cosmetic – *nuisances* or. Well – not – nuisances – (I – don't – know.)

JUDY. But you're trying to get pregnant //

CAROL. I'm just speaking editorially.

(beat)

MARTIN. You're so cynical.

CAROL. Well it's a cynical age and I'm the zeitgeist Let's get the check.

JUDY. (Well I want // kids.)

MARTIN. I just think you're full of shit. I do. I think you're full of shit.

(pause)

CAROL. *(terse smile) Well,* "charmed."

(She takes a sip of her drink. It's tense.)

JUDY. He doesn't really think that – Martin –

CAROL. Well we should really be going anyway, but thank you for dinner even though I'm full of shit and everything.

MARTIN. I'm sorry – I don't know why I'm so //

CAROL. It's OK – forget it,

MARTIN. I'm // sorry

CAROL. Stop apologizing it's redundant –

JUDY. *(damage control)* He's just stressed out.

JERRY. You know what we need old man, a good game of SQUASH.

MARTIN. What?

JERRY. Say, what are you doing *Mon*day.

MARTIN. Playing squash with you Jer.

JERRY. Splendid old man I'll reserve a court.

CAROL. Why are you stressed out?

MARTIN. I'm not stressed *out.*

CAROL. From the move?

JUDY. We're both. We're kind of exhausted ha ha ha –

JERRY. *(has been munching on petit fours all the while)* Oh this is GOOD, oh you have to TRY // these

CAROL. *(ignoring him; to* **MARTIN***)* Is the commute bad?

MARTIN. *(a discovery)* No //

CAROL. What do you take the Cross County? //

MARTIN. The Merritt //

CAROL. OH I heard the traffic's in*suff*erable //

MARTIN. There's //

CAROL. I told you not to leave the city, I mean I don't want to fingerwag but (well yes I do) HA HA HA (but it's –)

(As she wags her finger, JERRY *tries to feed* CAROL *a petit four. She keeps pushing him off.)*

JUDY. There's boxes everywhere.

CAROL. Why? – oh with *things* in them? Oh so you're still –

JUDY. We haven't finished unpacking.

CAROL. No THANK you Jerry.

*(*JERRY *eats the petit four.)*

JERRY. *(to* MARTIN *and* JUDY, *mouthful of food)* But you like it?

MARTIN. No.

JUDY. Yes we *do* – you're so *bad* honey. *(to* JERRY *and* CAROL*)* It's very quiet, it takes time to get used to the quiet.

CAROL. I can't get to sleep without the sound of jackhammers, the construction.

*(*JERRY *is trying to feed* CAROL *petit fours and she keeps pushing him away over the following.)*

(to JERRY*)* No *thank* you I don't like *almonds.*

JERRY. *(drunkenly)* Whatever you say darling.

CAROL. *(as he kisses her hand)* Don't do that.

JERRY. *(waggish)* I'm in your *thrall* darling I'm *helpless.*

(He eats. Brief pause.)

MARTIN. *(essaying courage)* You know – and I don't want to belabor the point but in China Carol //

CAROL. Mm //

MARTIN. If you get engaged to someone, in China //

CAROL. Yeah //

MARTIN. And they die before the wedding: you can still marry them.

CAROL. *(sotto voce)* Good for China.

(beat)

MARTIN. But don't you think that's interesting //

CAROL. (No) //

MARTIN. You can ask for their hand in death because the Chinese people believe that marriage is eternal, that it goes on forever //

CAROL. Well the Chinese believe in a lot of things going on forever, don't they, like certain forms of *torture*.

JERRY. But we'd like to be Chinese darling.

CAROL. Well I wouldn't like to be Chinese, I'm happy being American.

JERRY. Even though they're *eclipsing* us?

CAROL. Who //

JERRY. The CHINESE!!

CAROL. Oh bullshit.

JERRY. They are Carol, they're the new *empire*.

CAROL *(speaks quickly)* I love all this catastrophizing people do: "new empire" – people //

JERRY. Well //

CAROL. (It's such bullshit) people are so. I mean YES we're sinking – but the sinking can go on for eons and nothing changes, America was *always* middlebrow, it's *always* been vulgar, and people are so //

JUDY. But //

CAROL. And WE hold it up – "we" being the intelligentsia, the cultured elite, progressive thinkers!

JUDY. *(tickled)* Oh *Carol*, you're so elitist.

CAROL. Oh Judy, you're so annoying; HA HA HA HA. I'm just kidding. *(beat; she takes a sip of wine; then speaking briskly)* No but you know what we're like, we're like *barges:* and we're holding up these big pyramids of *garbage* – and for a couple hundred years it was OK – until one day the garbage started to *multiply*. And it got more fetid, and more awful. And the barges began to *sink* under the weight; and now we're all just SINKING. *(smiles, triumphal)* But sinking can go on for a long time, we can go on like this in*def*initely.

MARTIN. I don't know about *that*. //

CAROL. *(dismissive)* (Oh you don't know about *any*thing.) //

MARTIN. But isn't this the naive American fantasy – "Oh it'll all be OK" when you know it won't // be

CAROL. *(looking at him)* OK this is what I'm hearing *bluh bluh bluh* –

JUDY. *(plastering a smile)* That's a very negative way to look at things Martin.

MARTIN. Well that's how it is Judy empires rise and fall.

JUDY. I just think you're being *negative*. When you say things you're wishing for them, they're wishes? Or. Like in *Peter Pan*? you know like when that bird dies and all the children say "I believe, I believe." //

CAROL. What // bird

JUDY. Or no they clap //

CAROL. Tinkerbell?

JUDY. "I believe."

CAROL. It's not a bird, it's a // *fairy*.

JUDY. And also, I think it's a political thing.

> *(They all just look at her.* **JUDY** *turns five shades of purple.)*

CAROL. What.

JUDY. *(slightly unnerved)* What we were saying before about. You know – it's a political thing.

> *(They all wait for an explanation. The silence is unbearable.)*

It's like – the climate? You know what I mean?

CAROL. *No.*

JUDY. Well – I can't explain it.

CAROL. Well if you can't explain it then what are you talking about?

JUDY. I just – I know what I'm trying to say but I. I can't put it into words?

CAROL. *(fake, frozen smile)* Well Judy: do you know what thoughts are? Thoughts are little *words* you know that Judy and you *string* the words together and THAT'S how you get THOUGHTS; I mean if you don't have *words* you don't *have* thoughts.

JUDY. I have thoughts.

JERRY. She has thoughts Carol everyone // has

CAROL. I'm not *saying* she doesn't think, I'm saying she has no thoughts on this particular *issue* // as evidenced by.

JERRY. *(to* CAROL*)* Sometimes thoughts are a bit more nascent darling, a bit more – *unformed*; thoughts are delicate, they need time to gestate, like how the grit of sand inside the oyster becomes the pearl darling – you see? That – *nacreous* shell – right Judy?

*(*JUDY *just smiles, strained.)*

CAROL. *(mean)* Will you stop smiling! *(breaks out in unexpected, teasing laughter)* I'M JUST KIDDING!

JUDY. Oh.

(They laugh.)

You scared me!

(beat)

CAROL. *I* feel like a shell! Ha ha ha.

JUDY. Oh – ha ha // You're so bad. You're so FUNNY. You're so BAD // Carol

JERRY. "We bad" //

CAROL. *I* feel like a shell. *(beat)* HA HA HA I'm kidding.

JERRY. "We bad" what's that from

JUDY. ("We bad")

(She takes a sip of wine.)

I'm so full. I'm very full from the meal.

MARTIN. You hardly touched your fish.

JUDY. Well I'm on weight watchers.

CAROL. *Weight* watchers?

JUDY. I used up my points, hake is eight points and I had half.

CAROL. You don't need to lose weight.

MARTIN. I tell her that.

JUDY. *(sort of hysterical)* Well – I mean I feel simply *upholstered* in my dress, my clothes are so tight, it's all it's all stretched and – ruined My whole – wardrobe is...

[STOP]

JERRY. *(eating)* Well you know the *nice* thing about thin people Judy is they don't take up much room. And then there's so much *more* room for other *people. (He licks his fingers.)* I find them – *(mouthful of food)* very

(CAROL *waits for him to finish.*)

CAROL. *(to everyone; a good-bye)* Well it was // fun

JERRY. *(emphatic, drunken slurring)* and I mean – isn't this the WHOLE PROBLEM? I mean...people don't want to *know* each other: I mean – everyone *lurches* around, knocking into each other like little toy *cars*. And that's the problem with the whole world, And they're *lurching* all over the place! Th-Th-Th – Because people aren't *authentic*, that's the problem you know There's no *authenticity*. You know what I mean Martin, I mean *right?* And-nn-Er. you know they're all circling this – terrible abyss of uh uh pain. And – it's *our* job to get in*side* of that you see? because – I mean if we can't *enter* people's suffering then *we* suffer. Because we're disconnected from their lives: and *their* lives *are* our lives – but we don't want to *see* that. And then we in*flict* suffering!

JUDY. But – *whose* lives are our lives?

JERRY. *(gets lost for a moment)* Well just *every*one, what do you mean *WHO* //

CAROL. "Everyone" //

JERRY. The *Other* //

JUDY. Like, people in other countries? // or

JERRY. in *other* countries, in *this* country – in this *rest*aurant, they're suffering but no one wants to *enter* it But what can we do? what can I do What can *any* of us do I don't *know* I just keep *con*jugating the // problem!

CAROL. "enter their suffering" that's such *bullshit* you won't even let me use your *shampoo* //

JERRY. *because* darling // my *scalp*

CAROL. you won't even share your *toilet* articles with // *me*

JERRY. I have my – *flaking* – thing (anyway // it isn't the point)

CAROL. *(More vehement, focused)* and anyway these aren't benign – what do you THINK Jerry, you think the world is peopled with shepherds and milkmaids and they all //

JUDY. But //

CAROL. because in fact some people are evil.

JERRY. "evil"

CAROL. I know that's unfashionable but YEAH: *evil*, yes, they torture, they – look at these Christian Funda*men*talists //

JERRY. Well *actually* darling, if I may – because I actually think it would be sort of refreshing to get to experience some *real* fundamentalism here. Because – I'm glad you mention it Carol – because I'm feeling something of a *void* in this area Carol. Because my problem, er, if you want to know the truth…actually I'm glad you brought this up darling – because. *(His mind goes blank for an instant.)* I mean these *Christian* people: *(leaning in, wide-eyed)* they *say* they're fundamentalists but – where *is* the fundamentalism exactly? I mean I'm *looking*: I can't seem to *find* any. Is it under the *bed*? Where is it? Is it in the *cupboard*? Because they just sort of *make* things up – "oh we're fundamentalists" – but they don't actually know the first thing about Christ, or Christian love, not the first *thing*! I mean – where are the *fundaments*?! Right Judy?

JUDY. Well – I'm Jewish // – but I

JERRY. I mean maybe what we should do is go to the fundamentalists and say "Well all right: *you* think *you're* a fundamentalist? *I'll* show you who's the *real* fundamentalist!" *(turns to* **JUDY***)* do you see what I mean Julie?

JUDY. And then what?

*(***JERRY*** freezes.)*

JERRY. Well... I mean – we just – *stone* all the adulterers – you see and. Then we *execute* the uh. People who mix – *fabrics* – er – together – and // then

CAROL. *(to* **JERRY***)* You don't even go to *church* //

JERRY. because the *pews* darling – my *legs* – //

CAROL. I'm tired //

JERRY. Anyways you're missing the – whole *point* darling: the fundamentalists are *suffering*.

JUDY *(after a beat)* And...how's that?

JERRY. *(sways drunkenly for a bit as a proxy for contemplation)* Well...er – I mean they don't *know* it necessarily – but that's why they inflict it on other *people* – because that's what people do – It's all *unconscious*. *(drinks, shrugs)* It's like analysis. Actually you know It's *just* like analysis I mean these *patients* Julie – do you think I tell them what to *do*? Hmm? I don't tell them *anything*. I don't give any *advice* – I don't *talk*! I don't do *anything* – I just mirror them back to *themselves*. People can't *see* themselves, so you *hold* up the glass, the mirror – no arguments, no resistance... I'm just a little *enzyme* that helps it all along, you see?

*(***CAROL*** is looking blankly at* **JERRY***.)*

CAROL. And for this you charge two-fifty a session?

JERRY. The money is a guarantor of the *purity*, to not accept *money* darling that would just be errr *confusing* //

CAROL. *(sarcastic nodding)* Keep going maestro //

JERRY. (and I *have* a sliding scale Carol // I'm not)

CAROL. Well get your sliding scale Jerry and let's slide back to the Upper East Side it's getting late *(looks at her watch)* I need the check //

*(**CAROL** begins to retrieve her things, looks around for the waiter. Notices her ring is missing – looks around for it –)*

JUDY. *No*, it's your anniversary We're taking *you* // out!

CAROL. Where's my ring?

JUDY. Oh – I forgot I was holding it.

*(She takes it off and extends it to **CAROL**. **MARTIN** intercedes and takes the ring.)*

(He doesn't seem to be playing. Beat.)

CAROL. Can I have that.

(He looks at her.)

MARTIN. Why.

CAROL. Come on stop playing around.

MARTIN *(looks at her)* Do you know that you're full of *shit*.

    [STOP]

CAROL. Stop playing // around.

MARTIN. I'm not playing around.

    (beat)

CAROL. Can I have my ring please.

JUDY. Martin //

MARTIN. Shut up //

CAROL. Don't tell her to shut up.

JUDY. He's burnt // out

MARTIN. I TOLD YOU TO SHUT UP.

    [STOP]

CAROL. Can // I

MARTIN. Take it, here.

(He hands her the ring.)

(pause.)

You know what Judy?

You're that grit.

Not the pearl.

You're that unformed *thing*. That's what you are.

(**JUDY** *turns slowly to him.*)

JUDY *(starting to shake)* OK.

MARTIN. *(brutal)* IT'S NOT OK.

(beat)

CAROL. Martin, you're acting insane.

JUDY. I'm sorry // if I

MARTIN. I was promised a pearl and I got grit; now it's time for the *shucking*.

JUDY. We were having such a nice time.

MARTIN. Am I invisible to you? Judy? Am I having a nice time?

JUDY. Honey you're scaring me.

MARTIN. you think I'm going to hit you? Maybe I should – because it's what you want, and I don't want to disappoint you being that we're all in *love* and we're *married* and we're little strumming *lovebirds*, with honey just *dripping* off our beaks, RIGHT?

[STOP]

Because you're obviously a *masochist* Judy, so *why* do *(He shakes her once.)* I try to make things equal when I *love* you *so* much and I deny you – with all this *love* – your truest deepest wish? *(beat)* Why should I deny you Judy when I pledged my *life* to you? How could I do that?

JUDY. *(hysterical)* W-why why are y-you...

(**MARTIN** *leaves.*)

JERRY. *(drunk)* Remember Martin: squash next Monday!

JUDY. *(shaking uncontrollably)* Oh no.

CAROL. *(afraid to cause a scene)* It's all right, Judy – just //

JUDY. *(having trouble breathing)* "I believe."

CAROL. Are you...

JUDY. *(presses her hands to her temples, trying to quell the hysteria)*
I believe
I believe
I believe I believe I believe I bel –

(Loud music. We hear the chords, something punk, a wall of music, it cuts them off.)

[TITLE: "The Evildoers"]

(The space starts to transform; the chaos of the argument is parlayed into the transition. This should all have the tenor of ecstatic ritual – the seams of the play are starting to pull.)

(JERRY and **CAROL** *frantically undress and get into nightclothes.)*

(JUDY *walks offstage in tears.)*

(MARTIN *grabs a raincoat and puts it on.)*

(Thunder over music. Rain.)

(MARTIN *fetches a bucket of ice for champagne. He pours it over his head.)*

(Blackout.)

(The title cuts off and music cuts out into a five-second shockingly loud sample of a train speeding dangerously. This should feel rather jerky and unstable.)

[TITLE: "Strangers on a Train"]

(The lights snap on.)

2.

(Three in the morning. A week later.)

(CAROL and MARTIN are standing at the door of the Thernstroms' apartment. MARTIN is sopping wet, removing his coat. There's a frantic nervous energy.)

MARTIN. I *know* it's late I'm *sorry* // I

CAROL. It's fine Martin Are you kidding We were *worried* about you // are you

MARTIN. It's so late it's – what, I don't // have my

CAROL. Three //

MARTIN. *(guilt) Three!?* //

CAROL. No It's FINE I was up I was cleaning the oven //

MARTIN. I'm // so

CAROL. Let me get your – Look at you you're all // wet

MARTIN. Well //

CAROL. Do you think you have a fever?

MARTIN. No –

CAROL. How can you tell?

MARTIN. I just //

(He feels his head – she jerks his hand away, quickly feels his head.)

CAROL. (I don't think you have a fever) Sit DOWN (you need to rest) let me get you a blanket //

MARTIN. *(starts to move)* Alright //

CAROL. *Don't track mud!* //

MARTIN. Uh //

CAROL. We just had the floors waxed (hold on) *no actually:* (I'm sorry // could)

MARTIN. Oh –

CAROL. you just take your shoes off there's a shoe rack, right // over –

MARTIN. *(flips off shoes)* Sorry I'll clean // that

CAROL. No. NO Stop apologizing no it's just //

MARTIN. Uh. //

CAROL. We just we had the floors – well never mind, there's a blanket *(She gestures.)* yeah put that on. *(He does – he looks rather pitiable.)* Do you want something to drink?

MARTIN. No I'm all set, thanks.

[STOP]

CAROL. We have Coquilles St. Jacques from Fauchon I could reheat it.

MARTIN. Oh, no I'm not // hungry but

CAROL. You sure?

MARTIN. Yeah my stomach // feels

CAROL. (Do you want tums?) never // mind

MARTIN. I'm all set, Carol but thank you.

CAROL. Well. Anyway.

> *(Pause.* CAROL *takes a pastille, sucks on it. They look out.)*

That's a fake Franz Kline you like it?

JERRY. *(offstage)* "Maaaartin?"

> *(*JERRY *enters in his pajamas and slippers, holding a pipe. He's still drunk, and still charming.)*

Martin old man! *(to* CAROL*)* You didn't tell me Martin was here, when'd you *get* here?

MARTIN. I didn't mean to wake you Jerry //

JERRY. WAKE me, oh come on I have inSOMnia, (I have *dreadful* insomnia) HEY you know you missed the squash game!

MARTIN. I'm sorry –

JERRY. *(pouts)* I reserved the court and everything!

MARTIN. I know.

JERRY. Well I'm just glad you're OK.

MARTIN. Well thanks old man, I'm alright.

JERRY. "Old man" – you know I AM an old man

MARTIN. I found a gray hair! and not on my head,

JERRY. NOOOOOOO, you know where you get (**JERRY** *opens a couple of buttons on his pajama top.*) them first? look, you see right on the aureole, abutting the NIPPLE, you see?

MARTIN. Uh –

JERRY. You see that: now what do you make of THAT? *(He sighs.)* Well anyways…*(He closes his shirt and a button pops off.)* Oh, uh – will you sew this on darling.

CAROL. No //

JERRY. JESUS CHRIST –

(He slips on the floor, nearly – but doesn't fall. He drops his pipe.)

CAROL. We had the floors waxed.

JERRY. Oh the damn floors that's right – oh my GOD – wow – where's my pipe?

*(**MARTIN** finds it, hands it to him.)*

CAROL. Do you have to smoke?

*(**JERRY** lights up over the following:)*

JERRY. *(smiling tensely)* Darling, don't you want to go and put on some makeup or something.

CAROL. No.

MARTIN. I'm sorry, I – I feel // like I'm –

CAROL. Where's my virginia slims?

(She roots around for them.)

JERRY *(puffs away)* This is just like a *slumber* party.

CAROL. Isn't it.

JERRY. What are you looking for darling.

CAROL. My cigarettes, have you seen them?

JERRY. *(to **MARTIN**)* Carol thinks I look very "hung" in these pajamas.

(He looks down, puffing on his pipe, maybe snaps the waistband of his pajama bottoms.)

CAROL *(to **MARTIN**)* Have you spoken to Judy?

MARTIN. Well //

JERRY. Judy's fine //

CAROL. No she ISN'T fine, you know she // isn't.

JERRY. Don't you worry about Judy, Martin.

CAROL. She's on medication.

JERRY. She's doing much // better.

CAROL. She's taking fistfuls of pills, she had a breakdown, she was in bad shape, she isn't FINE.

MARTIN. What do you // mean she

JERRY. *(to* CAROL*)* She did not have a "breakdown," darling // she's

CAROL. Well that's what the doctor said.

JERRY. Well he's a hack, he wouldn't know a breakdown if he had one right in the goddamn mirror brushing his teeth // in the morning

CAROL. *(to* MARTIN*)* I told her she could stay with us, but she insisted on – anyway it's a big mess – but you're back, and it's fine – why don't you just call her.

MARTIN. I don't want to wake her.

CAROL. She's so distraught, Martin, really.

MARTIN. I don't really want to speak with her yet.

CAROL. But I think //

JERRY. He doesn't want to Carol.

CAROL. Why wouldn't he want to?

JERRY. Carol //

CAROL. I mean what are you doing at our door at three in the morning – I mean it's FINE, you have carte fucking *blanche.* Come here whenever you want.

MARTIN. Well I appreciate that.

CAROL. So are you having an affair, what? You're breaking up with // Judy?

JERRY. He's not having an // affair –

CAROL. Why, how do you know, are you two // colluding?

JERRY. *(disquisitive; holding forth)* Listen: Carol: the male *animal* is designed for adventure – he lusts, he is a creature of lust: this is the *quid pro quo* of the male animal, it's what men DO. It's in our DNA, that's just what we do –

CAROL. No you don't walk out on your wife to have some DNA-sequenced *adventure*.

MARTIN. That isn't it.

CAROL. And don't think I've forgotten what you said to Judy, how you called her grit, and you acted all fucking insane that night.

MARTIN. I apologized to Judy.

CAROL. She never mentioned that.

MARTIN. I apologized. I went through the ministrations of *guilt*, that night, after we got back.

CAROL. Well then.

MARTIN. And Judy felt better. And we went to bed. And Judy was sleeping next to me, she was in her little *fetal* position, with her little *toes* //

JERRY. *(sweet)* Awww //

MARTIN. *Digging* into me //

JERRY. *(awkward)* Oh –

MARTIN. and I couldn't sleep, I was still up*set*, something was *gnawing* at me and I thought: you know what, fuck this Judy, *I can't sleep* – I just thought I'd be gone a few hours – I got on the Metro North, I thought I'll take it a few stops, but then I just kept going…I got into the city and I just sort of…rode around. And this guy came on the subway and he sat across from me – he was staring at me, it was making me uncomfortable. And I didn't feel like getting up, so I thought, fine I'll stare him down.

(beat)

So I stared back.

(beat)

And then he did something very interesting.

(beat)

He reached down
into his pocket
and as he was reaching
he was looking
right at me, as if to...indicate...that this
reaching was
directed *towards*...me.

JERRY. In his pocket.

MARTIN. Yes. That somehow at the end of this seemingly enormous pocket was...me.

(beat)

JERRY. Why would he indicate to you that you were in his pocket?

CAROL. Sweetheart he was jerking off.

JERRY. *Oh.* Oh I *see.*

CAROL. I know all about this, it happens to girls all the time, men are always jerking off at you.

JERRY. On the subway? //

CAROL. (Well I take taxis) //

MARTIN. And then one thing led to another and...we were *kiss*ing.

JERRY. Were what?

MARTIN. Kissing. *(beat)* French kissing.

JERRY. *French* kissing?

MARTIN. It's something I always wanted to try...with...with another...

CAROL. *(confounded)* Why would you want to try THAT.

MARTIN. Because I. What do you mean "why" – I was curious.

(beat)

CAROL. Was your curiosity *satisfied?*

MARTIN. *(defensive)* No; it wasn't.

(short pause)

CAROL. Meaning //

MARTIN. What do you think.

> *(pause)*

> I should go.

> *(He doesn't move.)*

JERRY. Do you want another blanket, old man?

MARTIN. I'm warm now.

> *(beat)*

CAROL. So are you *gay* // or

MARTIN *(a retaliation) Yes!*

> *(silence)*

CAROL. Why did you lie.

MARTIN. I don't want to talk about it.

JERRY. *(Looks at* **CAROL***)* You don't have to.

> *(pause)*

MARTIN. It's stupid to feel ashamed, I know that, but I can't help it.

> *(pause)*

CAROL. So you're leaving Judy? This is the *sine qua non* right?

MARTIN. *(quiet)* Yeah.

CAROL. *(no emotion)* That's sad.

> *[STOP]*

> *(fillip of anger)* Don't you care about what happens to **JUDY**?

JERRY. Carol.

> *(silence)*

MARTIN. *(very vulnerable here)* He's an architect. He took me back to his brownstone. His wife was at a conference, but she came back today and I had to go. They have an understanding. *(suddenly, irrationally heartbroken)* So we can't be involved in an emotional way, just physical.

(pause)

(He looks up at them, his eyes brimming with tears.)
But I need more.
(Snap blackout.)

3.

(Later the same night. **MARTIN** *is set up with a blanket and sheets on the sofa. He's reading Updike's Couples against the glow of very soft lamplight.)*

*(***JERRY*** *sneakily enters, unseen by* **MARTIN***.)*

(He tiptoes drunkenly, until he's right behind **MARTIN***.)*

JERRY. Comfy?

MARTIN. Jesus you –

JERRY. Heh heh heh heh.

MARTIN. You scared me.

JERRY. You want another blanket something with a higher *threadcount* maybe. Carol's BIG on "threadcount."

MARTIN. I'm OK.

*(***JERRY*** *takes* **MARTIN** *'s book from him. Looks at the cover.)*

JERRY. *(sloshed)* Updike. Up-dike.

(beat)

He's prolific but that's not tantamount to good. That's not tantamount to SHIT. *(beat)* I don't even know what tantamount *means*, I just *say* these things, they *issue forth* from my lips and I KNOW that they're true, I have an instinct. And we can't dismiss our instincts, don't you agree, because it would be catastrophic – I mean the effect of that, of. *(beat)* And you can accept me can't you Martin, with my flaws, my foibles, my little peccadilloes, my little…my *things*; can't you?

MARTIN. Of course Jer.

JERRY. *HEY* – I really feel like a RÉMY you'd like a Rémy wouldn't you alright so I'll SIDLE up to the bar and – GET ONE – how's that I'll just –

(He tries to get up – stumbles.)

MARTIN. Jerry why don't you sit down //

JERRY. Am I keeping you up old man, I //

Martin *(going over to the bar)* You sit *down* and *I'll* get you a drink.

JERRY. Oh, yay, (well you really don't have to) I mean if you're sleepy, I really don't want to trouble you, you're a guest in our home.

MARTIN. It's fine Jer.

JERRY. Well that's kind of you Martin.

(He watches MARTIN prepare a drink.)

"Jer" I like that, the shorthand "Jer" but that's what friends are they're people who know each other's minds,

MARTIN. You like it neat right //

JERRY. and they speak in shorthand, glyphs, there's all kinds of – what //

MARTIN. You //

JERRY. That's perfect, that's just how I like it. Thank you Martin.

(beat)

She's a darling girl isn't she?

MARTIN. Who?

JERRY. Carol!

MARTIN. Oh.

JERRY. Don't you think?

MARTIN. Sure.

JERRY. And – you know; because we're having a *baby* and everything.

(beat)

MARTIN. She's *pregnant?*

JERRY. What? Oh, er – YES – oh you didn't //

MARTIN. When did THIS happen?

JERRY. I thought I //

MARTIN. Congratulations old man!

JERRY. My "issue," yes – You know what Freud says about babies – he compares *babies* you see to *feces,* it's rather

wacky, but he – means it in a good way, he's very –
People misunderSTAND Freud, he's just a nice – (oh
that's it for me, thanks old man, that's) – ha ha – oh
swell.

(holds up his glass)

"To my little feces!"

MARTIN. *(laughing)* Here here.

JERRY. HA HA HA "my feces"

HA HA HA

Oh

"Oy vey"

HA HA HA

(wiping tears from his eyes)

oh my goodness-I so-love-Freud

(sips drink)

its – it's pathological

(beat)

MARTIN. When's she due //

JERRY. I think the fall sometime.

MARTIN. It's fall now.

JERRY. OH: oh I mean next fall.

MARTIN. *(after a beat)* But, then she'd be pregnant for a *year.*

JERRY. Oh; well I-I-I *spring* or something //

(JERRY *sips his drink.)*

Carol's a lovely girl really. *(pause)* I mean it's not all
roses, she complains, she has complaints.

MARTIN. About?

JERRY. You know: well for instance about my sperm and
everything: she says it's too *chunky* – I mean al*right,*
it's not so well blended, but I eat avocados!! – I don't
know, something happened to me. But HEY: the stuff
works, chunky, smooth, who's complaining!

(Slaps him in the back. Beat. Sips drink.)

MARTIN *(excitedly)* Jerry. you're going to be a DADDY.

JERRY. *(weird baby voice)* "da da" heheheh //

MARTIN. How do you *feel?*

JERRY. Feel? *(thinks about it)* well I feel – frightened.

MARTIN. Why?

JERRY. Well

I'm not sure.

I feel OK right now Martin, with you here, I'm not frightened at this very moment.

MARTIN. Neither am I //

JERRY. *(screams)* BOO!

MARTIN. *(recoiling in shock)* AH!

JERRY. HAHAHAH //

MARTIN. HAHAHHAH //

JERRY. *(loud whisper)* Shhh (ha ha ha) shh let's – ho ho – let's not wake Carol.

MARTIN. All right.

(Another button on **JERRY***'s pajama top has fallen off.)*

JERRY *(pouty)* Oh, now the other, oh, the *button*, now I'll really have to – and these are my *best pair* of pajamas, they're my favorite, my favorite in the whole world...

(beat)

MARTIN. Nice nips Jer.

JERRY. Well thanks old man I like them too. Carol doesn't think they're –

*(***MARTIN*** lunges for* **JERRY***'s nipple and tweaks it.)*

OW!

*(***MARTIN*** jumps up, runs, trying to stifle his laughter.)*

You bastard.

*(***MARTIN*** laughs. ***JERRY*** tries to go after ***MARTIN*** and slips – benignly – on the waxed floor.)*

(pointing, laughing) You're a dead man. *(getting himself up again)* Oh these damn FLOORS.

MARTIN. This is just like boarding school all over again! //

JERRY. *Isn't //* it?

MARTIN. Remember when Phil waxed your ass // in the

JERRY. reMEMber? Martin, I felt that in the back of my *throat* for god's sake.

(*They laugh.*)

Oh, my salad days, what happened?

MARTIN. (*after a beat*) They wilted.

JERRY. (*tickled*) Wilted? Oh SHIT –

MARTIN. Ha ha.

JERRY. (*hits him*) Don't shit me!

MARTIN. Ow.

JERRY. Oh – er –

MARTIN. Ha ha ha ha.

(**JERRY** *laughs.*)

JERRY. You'll always have me Martin, you know that; I mean I don't care if you fuck *light fixtures.* Or. (well-that-sounds-like-a-bad-joke-but-//-you)

MARTIN. Thanks Jerry

JERRY. You keep looking up at the chandelier, I mean – fuck it if you want, fuck the bookshelf! Just don't spooj on my Freud seminars other than that ha ha ha HAHA. (*beat, then very sweetly, intimate*) I'm your friend. Alright? Truly. (*clutches his hand*) Truly and profoundly. (*Pause*) And drunkenly.

(**MARTIN** *removes his hand, smiles awkwardly.*)

(*long silence*)

(**MARTIN** *pulls an argyle sock from his pant's pocket.*)

(*pause*)

MARTIN. Look.

(**JERRY** *regards the sock. A pause.*)

JERRY. Is – that for me?

(long pause)

MARTIN. I took it.

(silence)

I'm pathetic, I took it from his – drawer.

(beat)

JERRY. *(drunk)* I need socks. My sock has a hole in it.

(long pause)

MARTIN. He...builds things?

(tiny smile to cover)

(very tiny) There were these...*Models?*...everywhere?

*(He looks at **JERRY**; a deep sadness, a plaintiveness unearthed.)*

JERRY. What's the matter old boy?

(pause)

MARTIN. I'm forty – I'm almost *forty*, my life is halfway done, and there's nothing *in it*. And it's too late for me // now

JERRY. It's not // too

MARTIN. *(coming apart here) Why* am I stealing socks from people's drawers, it's so – *stupid* – I'm *stupid*, I – I feel so – And I shouldn't I shouldn't feel this way – It's wrong to feel ashamed, it's *wrong*, but it's *embedded* in me, so deep, it's *lodged* in me – that's why I'm *stunted*. My feelings are – *stunted* – I – at work I walk around – in the cafeteria, everyone's smiling, they're – and I don't know what to do with my *hands*, I don't know how to stand – I'm *numb* –

JERRY. Shhh – now come on //

MARTIN. There are h-h- people – in the world – like *me* – they aren't crippled by – they have some kind of joy, they let themselves but I can't, why?

JERRY. Well, you've always been a little wound up.

MARTIN. I'm so fucked up…and Judy's so fucked up – and I can't just *leave* her like this – she can't take care of herself…

(He looks at JERRY, so deeply sad.)

JERRY. It's – its all going to – work out.

(MARTIN rises, wipes his tears quickly, decisively, starts to dress.)

MARTIN. I'm gonna go //

JERRY. Now? // er –

MARTIN. I'm gonna go back. // Maybe she'll

JERRY. You're getting all – riled up here old man – *(grabs his arm)* just – now hold *on* // here a minute –

MARTIN. *(throws him off)* DON'T TELL ME TO HOLD ON –

(JERRY looks at him. A pause. Quiet.)

Oh my god I'm being completely crazy. Jerry I'm sorry – I'm // so sorry.

JERRY. It's – fine old man, it's – fine – now:

MARTIN. What's wrong with me.

JERRY. You've had a rough week. Now why don't you have a seat on the old sofa? Hmmm? *(He pats it, smiles gingerly.)* Nice and comfy, all for you Martin

(He pats it a few more times. MARTIN reluctantly sits.)

(long pause)

MARTIN. I made a mistake. *(nods sadly)* I can't just leave her like this. // This is –

JERRY *(perfectly sanguine)* Everything is going to be just *fine* //

MARTIN. I'm being // *crazy*

JERRY. JUDY is going to be *fine.*

(A beat.)

(smiling, encouraging) Judy's like a little rubber *band* Martin She'll just "snap back" into place.

MARTIN. That isn't true.

(*Beat. Smile fades.*)

JERRY. Well maybe it isn't true. (*beat*) But you're not doing her a favor by *deferring* the pain, are you?

(*beat*)

Listen old man you're HELPING Judy. I mean yes she's suffering and it's hard – but suffering can be *good* for a person, you know, it's quite *tonic*, suffering.

MARTIN. How is it good?

JERRY. Well the pain, you know (*beat*) it's *cleansing* – it's like in the Bible you see, when Jesus, or someone, I think it was him, he says "suffer little children" – remember that?

[STOP]

Well he does. Because the suffering is *good, that's* why he says it, it's *cleansing*, it strips you down and – it's like those Russian dolls.

MARTIN. What dolls?

JERRY. You know those (*gestures*) you just keep removing the big ones until you get to the littlest doll, and that's the densest, best one, the little doll in the middle, it's like a little *nugget* – a nugget of *truth*. (*beat*) *Don't look at me like that*, I have a lot of good ideas! – I'm making a lot of *sense* here: now look: the pain, see, that helps you to strip it down, and you just strip strip strip – strip the whole business down, that's the thing about suffering, it breaks you *down* and it breaks you into *pieces*: and it's absolutely: *demo*cratic: it's a *democracy*. And then you become your authentic self, and you're a whole SELF! Like one of those dolls, like – a little errrr *crystal* of yourself. Now, don't you want that for Judy?

(**MARTIN** *nods.*)

And don't you want it for your*self*? (**MARTIN** *looks at him.*) You're on the path now Martin.

MARTIN. (*beat*) Am I?

JERRY. Listen, pain is just the beginning – it's the opening, you have to get inside the wound...don't you see? *(beat)* this is the *path.*

(pause)

MARTIN. Really?

JERRY. YES, you're figuring it all out now, just keep going. *(waves his hand along)*

MARTIN. But //

JERRY. Keep going! Do it for Judy, do it for Carol – for me! You're helping *everyone!*

MARTIN. How?

*(Beat. **JERRY** thinks about it a second.)*

JERRY. It's a ripple effect! "Suffer little children" – suffering makes you human.

MARTIN. It does?

JERRY. Oh yes, yes. Let me tell you something about Human, these *people,* no one knows what human is, because it's not what you think. *(beat)* You know what Christ says? "Love thine enemy."

MARTIN. Yeah

JERRY. Not your neighbor, but your *enemy.* You know why he says that?

MARTIN. Why?

*(**JERRY** leans in.)*

JERRY. It's a *code. (smiles and nods his head, eyebrows raised)* It's a very deep, *gnomic* thing you see. You can't love your enemy – it's a *non*sensical – you know – it makes no *sense,* you can't love someone you don't love – because you *hate them*! I mean that's a doomed enterprise don't you think? so why does he *say it* – and then he actually enjoins you to do it!

MARTIN. Is it because – that love is – that we're meant to // suffer?

JERRY. It's that *love* – ergo *human* – can't be what we *think*. *(beat) Real* love. *Christian* love. It's not about feelings – *feeling* love. It's deeper.

MARTIN. Like the Russian doll?

(**JERRY** *weaves drunkenly.*)

JERRY. Wha?

MARTIN. The – Russian // doll?

JERRY. Listen – Martin, you know these – subatomic *particles*?

MARTIN. What?

JERRY. Subatomic – you know – the – the //

MARTIN. You mean like – quarks?

JERRY. *Quarks* – yes! It's like *quarks*! I mean *quarks* – think about it, do they *dislike* other quarks? They don't have *enemies* – They don't have love, they just sit around being quarks and composing matter. Does a quark say, "I don't like that quark, I'm going to kill it, I'm going to rape it, I'm unhappy, I want a divorce." NO. because these things aren't real. And what could be MORE real than quarks? I mean – we fucking ARE quarks – that's how REAL they are, without quarks there could BE no human beings...do you see?

(pause)

MARTIN. So: Christ wants us to be like – *quarks*?

JERRY. *(shakes his head no – wobbling)* We ARE the quarks old man...

(**MARTIN** *looks at him.*)

MARTIN *(tentative)* I'm quarks.

JERRY. The *fundaments*!

(**MARTIN** *looks at him.*)

MARTIN. We're quarks.

JERRY. That's right.

MARTIN. And Christ...*wants* us to...*be* quarks – to *know* we're quarks //

JERRY. *(nods excitedly)* Keep going!

MARTIN. But we don't *know* we're the quarks because //

JERRY. Yeeesss?

MARTIN. Because – we think we're the Russian – *dolls*! – not the little one in the middle – the big clunky one on the *outside*. But – that doll's a lie! Right? We're not that doll...

(pause)

JERRY *(drunk)* The *Wha?*

MARTIN. Because – that's not the human...

JERRY *(sips)* Wha human?

MARTIN. And that's how you love your *Enemy*! by getting to that – *place* – inside the *molecules* //

JERRY. *(plastered beyond measure)* Strip-strip-strip!

MARTIN. and to do that...you have to enter their suffering... or else *you* suffer. *(a discovery)* Because it's all linked up. *(pause)* It's *one* thing.

(pause)

JERRY. "Suffer little children..."

(beat)

only in that case it doesn't mean "suffer" – I just remembered – it means something like "get over here."

MARTIN. *(mock anger)* "Get over here"!

(They laugh.)

JERRY. And when I was a runner, remember in high school Martin and I was running on that running team remember I would – I mean *god* knows – I mean – FUCK – I killed myself, sprinting, running, jumping I don't know what the fuck I // was HA HA

MARTIN. You were good too.

JERRY. I was, I was very fleet //

MARTIN. You were fast.

JERRY. And the pain in my calves every morning and *(beat)* and you know I *miss* that…without that *pain* there's – you know, you feel deprived…your life is…empty.

(**MARTIN** *studies him very intently.*)

MARTIN. Is that how you feel?

JERRY. *(snapping out of it)* What? No. NO no.
ha ha ha.

(He drinks; **MARTIN** *is staring at him.)*

Is something…the matter?

MARTIN. *(beat)* God, it's almost six I should try and get some sleep.

JERRY. Well – I won't keep you up with any more of my blather.

MARTIN. You're not keeping me up.

(**MARTIN** *looks in his eyes. Then looks away, discomfited.*)

JERRY. Martin?

(pause)

What is it?

MARTIN. Oh…nothing.

JERRY. What is it old man?

(beat)

MARTIN. You'll think I'm crazy.

JERRY. I won't think you're crazy.

(pause)

MARTIN. Well. I just. I think I went "inside the molecules."

(beat)

JERRY. You did NOT.

(**MARTIN** *nods.* **JERRY** *looks at him.)*

What happened?

(beat)

MARTIN. You seemed very…sad…to me…

JERRY. *Sad?*

> *(pause)*

> But – I'm alright – I'm not *sad,* I feel fine, in fact I'm in a very jocular MOOD.

MARTIN. No? – well all right, that's

JERRY. I *feel* fine…But you're saying I'm – sad…

MARTIN. It's all right – I think I'm going a little – *nuts* over here, it's been a long –

> *(He accidentally spills* **JERRY***'s drink.)*

> SHIT – I'll clean that –

> *(***JERRY*** *gets up –* **MARTIN** *stands, helps him.)*

JERRY. There's nothing wrong.

MARTIN. Is there a – do you have a rag or, or a //

JERRY *(smiling, drunk)* There's nothing wrong with me. Alright? If I were unhappy somehow if I were unhappy I would tell you, of course I would, you're my friend. You're my dear friend.

> *(***MARTIN** *nods, looks away.)*

> *(***MARTIN** *starts sobbing.)*

> *(***JERRY** *looks at him, sadly.)*

> *(consolingly)* Everything is OK.

> *(***MARTIN** *turns to him; he forces a tiny sympathetic smile.)*

> *(He touches* **JERRY***'s hair.)*

> *(He holds* **JERRY***'s face in his hand, with real love, and real empathy.)*

> *(He – and it's sudden – kisses* **JERRY** *fully on the mouth.)*

> *(***JERRY** *acquiesces briefly – then pulls away…)*

> Oh.

> Whoo.

(Beat. He smiles, musingly)

Gee. *(Beat. Amused)*

What do you think *that* was?

*(He laughs. He ribs **MARTIN**. **MARTIN** doesn't crack a smile, he seems worried. He looks away from **JERRY**.)*

(The sound of the train and whistle comes up and gets unbearably loud. Lights snap off; sound cuts out.)

End of Act One

ACT TWO

1.

(**JUDY** and **MARTIN**'s home in Fleetwood. The apartment is lit with candles.)

(Things are still in boxes, in neat stacks. Some of the boxes are opened, some not.)

(**CAROL** is munching on dried apricots, chain smoking virginia slims, reading to **JUDY** from Huxley's Brave New World.)

(**JUDY**'s hair has a shock of white in it.)

CAROL. "…and oh, oh at my breast, the little hands, the hunger, and that unspeakable, agonizing pleasure! Till at last my baby sleeps, my baby sleeps with a bubble of white milk at the corner of his mouth. My little baby sleeps." (Beat. Looks up) This is a rather reactionary little book isn't it. (slams the book shut)

JUDY. Keep reading //

(**CAROL** lights a cigarette.)

CAROL. But I've already read eight pages Judy and the typeface is so small //

JUDY. I haven't been read to in ages //

CAROL. Get books on tape, I find Alan Alda's tenor so soothing //

JUDY. Goodnight Moon //

CAROL. Martin got these for me, I don't know why, they're good, they're spiced with something //

JUDY. My father used to read to me

CAROL. *(munching on an apricot)* He's behaving rather strangely, him and Jerry, you should see them poring over Bibles it's driving me up a wall //

JUDY. *Goodnight Moon.*

CAROL. What?

JUDY. It's a book

CAROL. What is it some nuclear holocaust thing?

JUDY. (What) //

CAROL. It's so *country* up here. *(holds out bag of apricots)* Want some apricots.

JUDY. When do you give birth //

CAROL. I like your hair by the way.

JUDY. You should read it to the baby, I used to love that book.

CAROL. (Oh right I have to read it things) //

JUDY. When are you due?

CAROL. June something // it's in

JUDY. *June –*

CAROL. my palm pilot

    (beat)

JUDY. Do you want something to drink.

CAROL. You know I really like this hair thing, the shock of white, very Sontag.

JUDY. But she's dead.

CAROL. But you're immortalizing her *hair.*

JUDY. *(regarding* CAROL's *cigarette) Could you –*

CAROL *(puffing manically)* A few more puffs.

JUDY. You're pregnant?

CAROL. Yeah I don't know *(puff)* my mother smoked like a chimney when she had me. *(puff)* there was a lot of traffic getting here I was surprised. *(beat)* So what are you going to do?

JUDY. What am I //

CAROL. Are you going to sell this place, or //

JUDY. I don't know.

(*pause*)

CAROL (*brightly*) I have a friend who builds tract housing for millionaires he's lovely. He's the great-grandnephew of Gustav Klimt or something unbelievable like that, isn't that so snarky no but he's great, he's got these gorgeous eyelashes, I think he's gay, oh he's so annoying, why's everyone gay. (*Oops – a gaffe. Beat. Then brightly again.*) But I like what you've done with the place – kind of. (Well. the candles, I don't know) I mean – it's *nice* and everything but it's a bit goth for me.

JUDY. The electricity's not working.

CAROL. What's the problem.

JUDY. The wiring?

CAROL. Did you call the electrician?

JUDY. He said not to touch it, there was a blackout //

CAROL. Who?

JUDY. (*tiny stutter*) M-Martin was supposed // to

CAROL. Well call the electrician.

JUDY. It's fine.

CAROL. Is that *all* anyone ever says anymore, "It's *fine*"?

JUDY. (*unfocused*) He was kidnapped, it's a whole story and I don't have the patience to do anything about it just now

CAROL. The electrician was kidnapped?

JUDY. No, his daughter.

CAROL. How dreadful.

JUDY. Could you read some more, it was soothing.

CAROL. I could find you someone, I know electricians I think.

JUDY. I'm capable, I can find one.

CAROL. You're sure?

JUDY. This is teakwood isn't it lovely?

(**CAROL** *sees a book on the table. She opens it.*)

I started that in the hospital,

CAROL. What is it, some kind of art project?

JUDY. It's just pictures.

(CAROL opens it. She turns a few pages. She's aghast.)

I've been looking at articles and things, I'm very –

(pause)

I've been reading about Pol Pot, and about the Kurds? and – just all these…these political things, and I find it very compelling.

CAROL. It's a little – disturbing.

JUDY. Well. We all have to see disturbing things sometimes.

(CAROL flips through the book – slowly – registering shock. She looks at JUDY.)

CAROL. Your doctor's seen this?

(JUDY spontaneously begins to weep.)

JUDY. Now I – I feel ashamed.

CAROL. Why are you crying.

JUDY. *(covering)* Could I have that back?

CAROL. I think it's good you – have *proj*ects; I'm not saying feel *ashamed* –

JUDY. I'm not ashamed, it's – the light hurts my eyes.

CAROL. *(referring to the lack of light)* What light?

JUDY. And I'm not crying // I'm

CAROL. Judy you can't live without electricity, this is // ridiculous

JUDY. I don't want to argue //

CAROL. We're not arguing //

JUDY. *(vulnerably)* No – no because we *love* each other.

CAROL. *(flip)* I don't know about that, I'm just saying we're not arguing. HA HA HA I'm TEASING sweetheart.

(JUDY says nothing – she hasn't the mettle.)

(more gently) Maybe you should stay with your mother.

JUDY. No – she doesn't want me.

CAROL. Don't be martyry of course she *wants* you.

(**JUDY** *says nothing.*)

(*very gingerly*) I just think being up here like this, it's a bit...too...monastic; you need to be around other people.

(**JUDY** *looks at* **CAROL**, *tentative.*)

JUDY. The doctor? At the hospital? He said that I needed to *pretend* I had one good parent, that's what people do. But that my parents were both very – abusive //

CAROL. "Abusive"?

JUDY. To me? That's what he told me, we discussed it. He said people like to believe that they have one good parent, to feel safe, but it's not true.

CAROL. That sounds like forgive me but a bunch of claptrap //

JUDY. (*pleading*) And that that's why I married, I – I'm-m-m, that's why I got m-married? You know?

CAROL. Well I like your mother a tremendous lot, she has character // ("abusive," that's

JUDY. "Character."

CAROL. such textbook Freudian bullcrap.) //

JUDY. She //

CAROL. Mothers love their children, that's innate, it's a physiological thing (I mean yeah *some* of them drown their kids but) // that's –

JUDY. Well //

CAROL. Do you want an apricot? //

JUDY. that's what he. He told me my // parents were

CAROL. I'm not saying she's perfect, I'm saying she doesn't know any better, her parents were immigrants.

JUDY. (They weren't immigrants.)

CAROL. Well-she-speaks-with-that-accent //

JUDY. (No // she)

CAROL. (*impatient, rancor*) Well WHATEVER Judy – I'm just // saying

JUDY. I think – for right now? I should just be up here //
    and I

CAROL. Jerry said this guy was a hack, I don't think you
    should listen to him //

JUDY. Or –

CAROL. LISTEN: let's pack a few things, you'll come back
    with me in the hummer.

JUDY. I can't //

CAROL. Where's your suitcase //

JUDY. Could you please keep reading, you stopped and it
    was so *soothing* //

CAROL. We could go to La Goulue, they have that prix fixe,
    what time is it, I'll call your mum and we…

    (**JUDY** *fearfully nods "no".*)

Do you like it here? how could you like it here?

JUDY. *(sad)* I don't.

CAROL. No, you couldn't, because it's dreadful.

    (beat)

JUDY *(slow acknowledgment)* It's…dreadful. Yes.

CAROL. Then come on –

JUDY. I…hate it here.

CAROL. Darling

JUDY. I hate my life. I don't know what I'm doing, oh my
    god //

CAROL. But then it'll all flip around,

JUDY. Oh my GOD Carol.

CAROL. you just have to change it.

JUDY. *How, I can't –*

CAROL. You just have to know what you want, but you're
    too fucked up for that just now, OK sweetheart?

    (**JUDY** *absentmindedly opens her scrapbook.*)

JUDY. Did you know that in China there's a group called
    "Falun Gong," and the Chinese government wedges

like pieces of wood under their fingernails, they have these devices, they dig nails into – their – FACES //

CAROL. I don't want to talk about Falun Gong, let's just pack.

JUDY. And in Iran –

CAROL. *(abrupt; sarcasm)* And you're *like* all these people, *right?* you *identify* with them?

JUDY. *No //*

CAROL. Because your husband is a fag and he walked out on you so you're a torture victim!

JUDY. I // didn't

CAROL. Because let me tell you something you have a fabulous fucking life, and if you lived under Mao or Pol Pot or whoever the fuck you'd be really fucking sorry, it's not comparable, do you understand – I know you're having a hard time but really you must try to not be so florid about your grief: divorce is completely ordinary; *most* people get divorced, you're the status *quo* –

JUDY. Yes.

CAROL. If Jerry left *me* I wouldn't *care.* because my identity isn't based on my marriage, my own health has really pretty little to do with the health of my *marriage.* Just because the marriage is falling apart doesn't mean that *I'm* going to fall apart; so don't fall into that trap.

(She holds up the scrapbook.)

This: is not *you:* do you understand – these feelings are not *your* feelings, don't feed on this bullshit, it's pathetic.

(She rips up the book.)

[STOP]

What, don't look at me like that.

Here have an apricot.

JUDY. He got them for you.

CAROL. What.

JUDY. *(near tears)* He *got* them for YOU don't BRING them here.

(beat)

CAROL. Judy //

JUDY. You're *living* with him…you *see* him, do I want to KNOW about that?

CAROL. Well what do you want me to do // Judy

JUDY. Just put those away please.

CAROL. They're APRICOTS //

JUDY. *(shaken)* PUT THEM AWAY.

(CAROL puts the apricots in her bag – shuts it with a histrionic clang.)

CAROL. Remember that thing when you stood too near to that Chuck Close painting and that thing in your brain happened well *I'm having that now.*

[STOP]

JUDY. You're…just like her.

(CAROL starts packing.)

CAROL. This is a cute top, where'd you get this, Barneys Co-Op?

JUDY. I don't know how I never saw it.

CAROL. (Saw what) I like the decolletage //

JUDY. You're like her…you're like my mother.

CAROL. Why because I'm *abusive?* Is mother code now for "abusive"? Did they do like reverse neuro-linguistic *pro*gramming on you // Judy?

JUDY. Please put that back, I'm not coming with you.

(JUDY takes the sweater.)

CAROL. How am I abusive? *(pulls the sweater back)* Oh, you're being unreasonable. And your mother loves you Judy she's just a little – *stalwart.*

(CAROL resumes packing for her – then stops abruptly.)

JUDY. *She'd* come here, and *she'd* rip up my things //

CAROL. Come ON //

JUDY. and *she'd* drag me around, and force me to wear her horrible // scarves

CAROL. Judy //

JUDY. and she'd say it was because *she* loved me.

CAROL. She does love you.

JUDY. She can't stand me.

CAROL. Are you saying *I* can't stand me – *I mean YOU.*

JUDY. Put that back please.

CAROL. You're coming with // me –

JUDY. "Yes mother" //

CAROL. OK the mother thing is freaking me out – I'm starting to have second thoughts, maybe I should uh – ABORT?!? I mean – uh – ha ha – uh…

(**CAROL** *resumes packing.*)

JUDY. Maybe you should.

(*She turns to* **JUDY**, *who's serious.*)

CAROL. *Well thanks.*

JUDY (*earnestly*) I think that as a mother you'd be a catastrophe.

(*pause*)

(**CAROL** *laughs – thinking this is a joke. Oh – it's not a joke.*)

CAROL. I have a meeting.

JUDY. Yes; go to your meeting.

(*pause*)

CAROL. I have to be back in the city.

(**CAROL** *looks at her, worriedly.*)

Are you sure you…

(**JUDY** *looks out.*)

(**CAROL** *hesitates, then gets her things. She exits.*)

(Music in:)

(**JUDY** *smiles softly, a strange, sad smile, as the tears come.)*

[TITLE: "The Fright of Real Tears"]

2.

*(The Thernstroms' apartment. Thanksgiving Eve
– MARTIN, JERRY and CAROL are all having a
traditional Thanksgiving dinner. MARTIN is wearing a
pink oxford shirt, his hair is slicked back. It should all
register as a little too proleptically "gay" – he's getting
ahead of himself. The rhythms here should be fast and
furious.)*

CAROL. Pass the yams //

MARTIN. And she and then // she

JERRY. And where were you?

MARTIN. I'm –

JERRY. *(remembering)* (Yes yes yes yes yes) //

MARTIN. She ripped off a piece of the duct tape //

JERRY. The mother //

MARTIN. Uh-huh and she put it on the girl's mouth, and
she ripped it off and the daughter had these tears –
she had these // tears

CAROL. Pass the yams.

MARTIN. And the girl says I'm going to TELL them what
you do to me and the mother says who's going to
believe you who's going to believe YOU //

JERRY. *(pouring wine for MARTIN)* You –

MARTIN. (No no) and the daughter. Uh. had these pink
eyes it was //

JERRY. Well //

MARTIN. Do you know what that means?

CAROL. Jerry isn't wearing his secret decoder ring right
now? so // I don't think

JERRY. Carol //

MARTIN. I'm sorry is this tedious I shouldn't be belaboring
– I'm sure everyone comes to you with their dreams.

JERRY. Not Carol //

CAROL. Because I don't dream.

MARTIN. Everybody dreams.

JERRY. You don't REMEMBER // your dreams

CAROL. *(to JERRY)* (Stop picking your eyebrows) //

MARTIN. If you don't dream you go insane.

CAROL. Hence: my life. HA HA HA.

JERRY. *(squeezing her arm)* Now // daarlling

CAROL. What, *no* (stop clawing me) don't // spill that

JERRY. *(sings quietly)* "You made me me love // you"
     (da da da da da da do do do do...)

MARTIN. These brussel // sprouts are

CAROL. Oh you like those I got the recipe from Mario
     Batali it's – you roast them it's really easy.

JERRY. How are you feeling darling?

CAROL. I'm a little sick actually,

JERRY. Maybe you should //

CAROL. *(to MARTIN)* You know *yams* are a *superfood* //

MARTIN. Really

CAROL. they have lots of minerals, yams, they're superfoods,
     lots of vitamins and they're // so

MARTIN. *(to JERRY)* I guess //

CAROL. They're // so

MARTIN. I mean the idea of feeling stifled, that you won't
     be HEARD: that's part of it.

JERRY. Uh –

MARTIN. The dream?

JERRY. Oh!

MARTIN. And in a way it's like – and there was violence,
     and this kid //

CAROL. And cruciferous vegetables.

MARTIN. I'm sure –

JERRY. *(to CAROL)* What's that dear?

CAROL. Cruciferous vegetables, those are superfoods.

JERRY. They're shaped like little crucifixes //

MARTIN. *(non sequitur)* As a gay man, I mean *that's what's so
// exhilarating* –

CAROL. *(noticing her ring is gone)* Where's //

MARTIN. that I'm – I'm not *that* – because that's what I've
come to realize, that there's no silver bullet, that's the
thing, no *shortcut,* that's the problem with. Or maybe
there *is* a shortcut but if you *take* one you'll never get
there, you have to enter the wound.

CAROL. Where's my //

JERRY. Did you say something darling?

CAROL. My ring, I had it right on my – you didn't do
anything with //

JERRY. No darling no I // didn't –

CAROL. Well where is it WHERE IS IT?

JERRY. Well we'll find it we'll FIND //

MARTIN. *(finds it)* Bingo

JERRY. Darling here it is, here it is –

CAROL. Now how did that –

MARTIN. Right here //

CAROL. I took it off that's right, oh thank you Martin.

(pause)

MARTIN. It's so interesting Carol.

CAROL. What's that Martin.

MARTIN. This attachment you have to – well now it's a
piece of costume jewelry but. Well it's not a part of
your history anymore, you can see that can't you it's
just a pretty *thing.*

CAROL *(taut smile)* Well it really isn't and you're sweet but
any of your business.

MARTIN. I'm just //

CAROL. So let's terminate the conversation now shall we.
(beat) and while we're at it you really aren't a paragon
for marital happiness –

MARTIN. *(not ceding the ring)* No I'm not –

CAROL. Can I have that back?

(He holds the ring out to her; she puts it on.)

MARTIN. I'm just super sensitive right now, I'm sensitive to things because MY situation is so unstable.

CAROL. Well some systems tend toward entropy. *(beat)* Speaking of which Martin what is your plan?

MARTIN. For…

CAROL. Your situation? do you have a plan? or //

MARTIN. A plan //

CAROL. For your life?

MARTIN. *(after a beat)* Well I'm still trying to…orient myself…

CAROL. *(beat)* So your plan is to be *oriented?*

MARTIN *(laughing)* Well // no –

CAROL. No, that's legitimate, that's a legitimate goal, we all need to be oriented, I mean we can't go around smacking into walls, that's not a way to live. *(beat)* Well good.

JERRY. *(picking out his eyebrows yet again)* Martin's just – figuring it out right old man.

CAROL. *(pulling **JERRY**'s hand away)* STOP THAT //

JERRY. I'm not. They just fall out //

CAROL. (Your // *eye*brows)

JERRY. *(pouring more wine)* I *know* Carol "the pillars of the face" I know but // I don't

MARTIN. And Carol I know I've hurt Judy, I'm *not* saying I'm a paragon // of

CAROL. No no no DON'T exculpate yourself here all right // let me tell

MARTIN. I'm not –

CAROL. you something you don't give a shit about Judy: you haven't seen her, you haven't talked anything through. And you're avoiding the situation you aren't being brave you aren't honest you're a coward So spare me the sanctimony.

(pause)

MARTIN. *(meaning it, or wanting to)* Thank you. You're right. I am a coward. Thank you Carol – I'm – inching towards // my progress.

CAROL. And you have this CREEPY actually fixation on my engagement ring I // mean

JERRY. I don't think it's creepy //

CAROL. Well it is //

MARTIN. I'm just trying to understand you, I'm trying to understand the kind of person you are.

CAROL. *(eating)* And what kind of person is that.

*(She waits for a response. **MARTIN** does not respond. He eats. She looks up at him.)*

*(**CAROL** laughs, pretending to be cavalier.)*

You know I can see it now.

MARTIN. What.

CAROL. *(drops the smile)* The Jewishness, you have that. Uh. *Hebraic* severity. *(beat)* And Jewish people like to repeat things don't they, oh that's funny I see it now. *(She eats.)* The repetition – that's where that must come from – it's that *Talmud* thing isn't it, the endless regurgitation. You're. *(She chews.)* So exhaustive.

(She eats. This is uncomfortable.)

MARTIN. You know Carol you're incredibly privileged: you're having a *kid*, and you have a *marriage*, you – can I get married? no //

CAROL. Go to Massachusetts //

MARTIN. And you have a LIFE – I have a "lifestyle" – I have a "gay // lifestyle"

CAROL. Oh come on you're not some Stonewall hag from 1952 // Martin

MARTIN. I mean – my "plan" Carol I don't know – you tell ME – what IS it? What the hell am I doing, I don't know what to "plan" get a place in Chelsea and fuck people in it all day, is that a plan? //

CAROL. (It's more an itinerary but sure) //

MARTIN. Well I don't want to just fuck all right I want to fall in love. And I want reciprocal affection and I want to be *married*. And I know it means so *paltry* little to you, but it's what I *want*.

(**JERRY** *starts to play his game boy at the table.*)

CAROL. What you *want?* You *had* it.

JERRY. Gay people can fall in *love* // Martin

CAROL. (*grabs his Game boy*) (stop // that)

MARTIN. We can't get married – *not really* – because they – because *we're* – monsters evidently We need to be deprived of human connection –

CAROL. Well whining isn't going to help

MARTIN. I'm not WHINING if // anything I'm

CAROL. Maybe if you'd SHUT UP and take some ACTION for a change // you'd

MARTIN. (*deliberacy*) But I've taken. *Action* Carol.

CAROL. What's that supposed to fucking mean.

MARTIN. You'll find out what it means.

(**JERRY** *shifts uncomfortably. Smiles weakly – an attempt to leaven things, but is vanquished by all the bad vibes at the table.* **CAROL** *casually takes a bite of food.*)

CAROL. (*shifting tactics*) So how long have you been harboring these feelings, have you always been gay?

MARTIN. I'm. I'm not sure.

CAROL. How could you not be sure?

MARTIN. It's a hard question.

CAROL. It isn't actually, when you fantasized about sex was it with a *penis* or a *vagina?*

MARTIN. Neither.

CAROL. Because you never had sexual *feelings?*

MARTIN. Everyone has // sexual feelings

CAROL. I'm just curious, when does it become a salient piece of information: "I'm gay."

JERRY. He was repressing // it

CAROL. I mean say in boarding school, when you two were in boarding school, you were post-pubescent then, so what were your fantasies?

MARTIN. *(flustered)* I. I was busy – studying, I don't know.

CAROL. But what about when you weren't studying, like after gym class, in the showers, I've read stories.

MARTIN. I //

CAROL. Did you think of being penetrated? By a man?

(pause)

MARTIN *(not looking at her)* What if I did.

CAROL. Don't get angry // I'm just

MARTIN. Yeah so what. So men can be // penetrated

CAROL. I don't think it's a big *deal* I'm just asking: "*Have* you *ever* been *penetrated?* Do you ever think about that, being *penetrated?*" *(beat, smiling nefariously)* This is like curling up with a good *book!*

[STOP]

MARTIN. And have you *noticed,* have you noticed how *gay* people, how we're not actually *real?*

CAROL. You didn't answer my // question

MARTIN. How we're like these *golems* these *monsters* //

CAROL. Martin //

JERRY. You're not GOLEMS // Martin

CAROL. YOU DIDN'T // ANSWER

MARTIN. How we're like these – *hairdressers* these people on sitcoms // it

JERRY. But that's //

MARTIN. *(spasm of real anger)* I'm not your fucking hairdresser you know and it's like CUT YOUR OWN FUCKING HAIR.

(He slams down his fork.)

(pause)

JERRY. Now **MARTIN** you're just, you're up*set.*

(pause)

MARTIN. But I'm not upset. I'm invigorated;

JERRY. Are you?

MARTIN. I'm elated. *(pause)* Everything is just as it should be.

JERRY. *(drunk smile)* Is it?

(**MARTIN** *smiles warmly.*)

MARTIN. "Hold up the glass"…right?

(**JERRY** *smiles back reflexively. Then appears rather confused as he goes back to eating his stuffing.*)

JERRY. The wha – ?

MARTIN. The mirror. "Hold up the glass"?

CAROL. I'm still waiting for an answer to my *penetration* question but take your time. *(Beat)* Cute top by the way.

(**MARTIN** *glowers at* **CAROL.** **JERRY** *takes a big gulp of wine.*)

JERRY. *(musingly, a non sequitur)* "Love thy neighbor!"

(**CAROL** *gives him a dirty look.*)

(I'm just musing darling, jus' musing. Just…cogitating sweetheart. *(playful revision)* EX-cogitating! *(lifts a finger for emphasis)*

(**JERRY** *eats. A short pause.*)

CAROL. Actually it's "love thy neighbor as *thyself.*"

JERRY. Wha? Oh – well – that's a transLATION darling.

(She smiles diabolically.)

CAROL. But that's what it translates TO Jerry. That means you can *hate* your neighbor.

JERRY. Noooooo –

CAROL. YES you CAN that's what it en*dor*ses you can fucking *loathe* your neighbor as long as you hate your*self*! //

MARTIN. Actually in Christian theology it's "love your *enemy.*"

JERRY. That's true old man That's a good point – you *see* Carol Christ doesn't let you off so easy.

CAROL. *Where* does it say that.

JERRY. *(playful; wagging finger)* Someone has been neglecting her scripture *darling*.

(JERRY rises from his seat.)

MARTIN. "And it was said, an eye for an eye and // a tooth for a tooth;"

CAROL. Where are you going Sit // down

MARTIN. *(impassioned swelling of feeling)* "but I say unto // you:"

CAROL. Jerry //

MARTIN. *(pushes away from the table and stands)* "resist *not* The Evildoers" //

CAROL. *(to MARTIN)* SHUT UP!

(MARTIN stands, a fervid prayer, a plea.)

MARTIN. "And it was // said thou shalt love thy neighbor"

CAROL. *(to JERRY)* Don't open that //

(JERRY produces a Bible.)

MARTIN. "and hate thine enemy! But I say unto you: *love* your enemies, *bless* them that // curse you,"

CAROL. *(to JERRY)* SIT down.

MARTIN. "do *good* to them that // *hate* you – "

JERRY. Don't be so peremptory.

CAROL. YOU OPEN THAT I'LL FUCKING SMACK YOU IN THE HEAD!

JERRY. *(opens the cover, smiling)* Calm down darling –

(She smacks him. Hard. A beat.)

(JERRY turns the other cheek.)

(CAROL sits.)

(long pause)

MARTIN *(tiny smile)* It works…

JERRY. What's that?

MARTIN. *Quarks.*

JERRY. What? Err – oh sure, yes –

CAROL. What the hell are *quarks?*

JERRY. *(innocently)* They're little *particles* sweetheart.

CAROL. I KNOW WHAT THEY FUCKING ARE, I'M NOT –

[STOP]

(frustrated, to **JERRY***)* It's Thanks*giving*: I'm *preg*nant: we're having // a *ba*by

MARTIN. If you want to be authentic in your Thanksgiving: I mean what *is* Thanksgiving?

CAROL. GENOCIDE yeah I KNOW but I don't want to be *authentic //* Martin

MARTIN. But //

CAROL. I want to eat my Chambord cranberries and watch SPORTS!

[STOP]

MARTIN. You're so *American //*

CAROL. Yeah I AM "American" – and I *accept* it I *love* my country (and I know it's garbage but that doesn't stop // me from)

MARTIN. If you *really* embrace your country Carol you'd see that it has to break.

CAROL. "break."

MARTIN. Before it moves forward.

CAROL. Well that *won't* happen.

MARTIN. Really, it won't? Look at the Roman // Empire

CAROL. *(mimicking)* ("the Roman Empire The Roman Em") – *have you ever read* GIBBON Martin? Do you know how LONG the Roman Empire in fact *lasted?*

MARTIN. Empires // fall

CAROL. It lasted for-fucking-EVER and they were HORRIBLY corrupt they had *slaves,* they – you know not everyone gets this swift comeuppance, that's storybook bullshit.

MARTIN. Should you be drinking //

CAROL. Rhetorical questions are accusations Martin // YES I

MARTIN. I //

CAROL. SHOULD BE DRINKING Have you ever been pregnant? how do you think women endure pregnancy, I feel like a marsupial, I hate my *pouch*, my hips are cracking open –

MARTIN. Do you *not* want to be pregnant?

JERRY. Carol //

CAROL. Where's my // pulpit!

JERRY. Carol the // baby

CAROL. OK: wait what's this:

(She starts reading from the Book of Revelation 9:2, a mock-sermon:)

AND HE OPENED THE BOTTOMLESS PIT; AND THERE AROSE A SMOKE OUT OF THE PIT, AS THE SMOKE OF A GREAT FURNACE: AND THE SUN AND THE AIR WERE DARKENED BY – *REASON* AND – BY THE –

(She stops abruptly – she falls against the table.)

JERRY. *Darling?*

CAROL. I don't feel right –

(JERRY *runs to her;* **MARTIN** *is completely still.)*

(clutching her stomach)

I don't FUCKING. FEEL RIGHT –

(Snap blackout.)

3.

(The following morning.)

*(**MARTIN** and **JERRY** are both in their pajamas.)*

(Breakfast.)

(long silence)

*(**CAROL** enters, fully dressed.)*

CAROL *(no affect)* I'm going shopping.

JERRY. Darling…did you just…wake up or…

CAROL. I was doing the bills.

JERRY. Don't you think you should maybe…take it easy.

CAROL. I'm meeting Vera Wang at two, I'm doing that wedding upstate.

(She gets her things together.)

MARTIN. How do you…feel?

CAROL. *(snaps)* Maybe that's something you should ask Judy.

(beat)

JERRY *(quietly, uncomfortably)* Carol, Martin…was…just //

CAROL. *(glares at **MARTIN**, gelid)* When are you leaving.

(pause)

MARTIN. I //

JERRY. He has nowhere to go Carol – he's //

CAROL. *(curt)* OK *Jerry*.

(resumes putting lipsticks and things into her bag)

JERRY. What are you…going to –

*(She exits, we hear the door slam. **JERRY** sits very still, dejected.)*

(silence)

MARTIN. How is everything.

JERRY. What oh, delicious. Just delicious Martin thank you.

 (beat)

 I mean – I don't like poached eggs. But –

MARTIN. I thought –

JERRY. I really don't like anything. So – but I'll EAT anything, just put a plate in front of me: see? "mm, delicious!"

MARTIN. Would you rather have them scrambled, I could //

JERRY. No, no. it's just – I don't seem to like anything. I don't seem to have tastes.

 (short pause) Do you know: I keep a little notebook about the things I'm supposed to know, about Prokofiev, and what he did and William James and what he thought, but: I looked through my notebooks: I can't decipher anything I write. I mean I'm not kidding, it's like I've written everything in some kind of *cuneiform.*

 (He laughs; then "bright":)

 Gee, it's sort of interesting when you think about it old man: I mean you could draw out my complexity on a piece of *butcher* paper *(more frightening laughter)* with one of those those red – those *pen*cils, I mean //

MARTIN. It's sad to lose a baby.

 *(***JERRY*** nods. Pause. ***MARTIN*** looks at him, deeply sympathetic.)*

JERRY. Remember Roddy – he built that *bomb* in eleventh grade he was always reading that per*ni*cious literature?

MARTIN. What about him?

JERRY. Well now he builds bombs for a *living*, I ran into him //

MARTIN. Does he //

JERRY. Yes, that pig, he's in fucking MUNITIONS, the scum, and he makes an e*nor*mous amount of money, he works for the *gov*ernment. And I would have these conversations with him, late-night conversations

– when he wasn't leafing through one of his pernicious little books which he nearly always was. And we would have these arguments about the nature of the "self." And Roddy of *course* didn't believe that people had selves, he didn't think there WAS a self! He accused me of being gram*mat*ical! And I would say, "Well Roddy, if there's no self who listens to the *Quadrophenia* album, day after day, tormenting us all with your fucking aha ha *Quadrophenia* album? who is this *person*, Roddy?"

(pause)

And now it's all these years later and I'm sure I have *no...idea* what I was talking about and I'm sure RODDY has the most fanTASTic little life making bombs and eating those fried things with powdered sugar with his little freckled twins off some coast of something or other, and I'm completely...lost. *(beat; then sunny)* Well not *completely* lost ha ha, just, a bit uh, adrift, *(manic convulsion)* JUST A LITTLE. *(sober)* shall we say...

(JERRY covers his face. Pause.)

MARTIN. *(sadly, full of compassion)* Jerry.

(MARTIN goes to him, to console him. He wraps his arms around him. JERRY is very vulnerable. JERRY buries his face in MARTIN's shoulders. MARTIN is very moved. After a while, MARTIN lifts JERRY's head with his hands, he kisses the tears streaming from his eyes. JERRY lets him – it's the only love he's gotten in a very long time. MARTIN then kisses JERRY fully on the lips.)

(JERRY, disoriented, also a little disgusted, pulls away, uncomfortable – the trance is broken. This is too much.)

JERRY. No-no. *No* Martin.

MARTIN. OK.

JERRY. *(backing away)* Unh-uh. *(beat)* No.

MARTIN. OK I'm sorry.

JERRY *(very VERY shaken)* That's all right – th-that's – *(contriving a smile)* perfectly all right Martin, it's – it's natural. I mean for you.

MARTIN. There's many different kinds of love. I'm. just learning.

JERRY. Yes.

(pause)

MARTIN. Or maybe there's *one* kind of love but in different pitches, different frequencies...You just have to know how to listen for it.

JERRY. *(very shaken, speaking quickly, anxious)* Well it's *in*teresting, because – you know what li*bi*do is don't you Martin well, *Freud*, you see, he had these *(wiping tears, recovering)* these *in*teresting – ideas about libidinal *en*ergies – ca*thex*es he called them, I could – give you... literature if you...

(silence)

(As **JERRY** *is speaking* **MARTIN** *grows more and more faraway, lost in contemplation.)*

MARTIN. Do you know what the opposite of sin is? I thought it was virtue. But it's not virtue, do you know what it is?

*(***JERRY** *says nothing.)*

It's faith. *Faith.* *(beat)* And you get it by having a principle. You don't have to feel anything. Real love has nothing to do with feelings. It's deeper than that. You don't even have to believe, you just have to perform a series of actions. "If you kneel down and pray, the faith will come." That's why I'm doing all this.

JERRY. Doing all what?

*(***MARTIN***'s face lights up; he looks at* **JERRY** *expectantly.)*

MARTIN. Christian love...remember? *(short pause)* Just now I was trying to help you by comforting you, but that's not help. When you comfort someone, it's because deep down you feel there's no hope. That's how I used to feel...*(moved)* But now I know there *is* hope. But I'm still – all this old fake *stuff* – I'm still trying to root it // out

JERRY. To *comfort* me is all right, Martin it's // just

MARTIN. *(suddenly very focused, very intent)* You're at the portal and you're so scared but you have to enter into it. *(beat)* If I were just an ordinary friend I don't know maybe I could leave it alone...But you're *everything* to me. *(upset)* I won't let you die.

JERRY. *(perplexed; smiling)* Die? I'm not dying.

(**MARTIN** *looks at him with all the pathos and heartbreak one would feel toward a dying man oblivious to his own condition.*)

MARTIN *(a wounded child)* But...your soul is sick.

JERRY. My...*soul?*

MARTIN. *(quietly)* I didn't know until I came here. But I know it now.

JERRY. My *soul* is...sick?

(**JERRY** *laughs. The laughter builds. The more he laughs the more he wounds* **MARTIN**, *who looks on, helpless.*)

MARTIN. Do you know I hated myself ? That's why I chose my life. I chose a life I could hate so it could fit how I felt about myself. Is that what you're doing?

(**JERRY***'s laughter dies down. The embers of a smile over the following:*)

JERRY *(lying)* No.

MARTIN. *(rueful, deep sadness)* Jerry; you haven't suffered enough or you wouldn't be lying to me now.

(very tender, sweetly:)

I'm inside the molecules I can feel everything you feel, look at me: *this* is what you *look* like.

(**MARTIN** *looks right at him. He weeps openly.*)

JERRY. *(uncomfortable)* Martin – please
(feeling increasingly bad for him) Martin...
what are you...doing?

MARTIN. *Showing* you your *in*sides //

JERRY. *(uncomfortable)* Well stop it

  (stop; unexpected jolt of anger)

  STOP IT!

  (then retracts; he goes to **MARTIN***)*

  Martin please...

MARTIN *(weeping)* How do I stop? How?

  *(*JERRY *softens somewhat. He goes over to* MARTIN, *tentative, tousles his hair lightly.* MARTIN *lunges impulsively for* JERRY, *kissing him.* JERRY *pulls away. He wipes his mouth with the back of his hand.)*

JERRY. Don't do that!

MARTIN. Why?

JERRY. Why, because it makes me fucking UNCOMFORTABLE buddy, *that's* why //

MARTIN. But isn't discomfort a good thing? without discomfort you couldn't grow or change, you can't be a whole PERSON //

JERRY. But uh, that's marvelous and everything like that but: I'm *married* you see I'm married to Carol //

MARTIN. Married?

JERRY. Yes // *married*:

MARTIN. You don't even know who Carol *is*. You have no cognizance // of

JERRY. *(unstable)* Well, aha ha – OK but now – I mean I'm not GAY! I mean – orientation-wise, it's just, you know, it's not my THING. *(pause; then quietly pleading)* We're FRIENDS that's important to me I *need* your friendship...

  (beat)

MARTIN. I know...

JERRY. I lost a *baby*.

MARTIN. *(rueful)* And it wasn't enough.

  *(*JERRY *looks at* MARTIN, *flummoxed and deeply hurt.)*

JERRY. Don't do this; don't scare me like //

MARTIN. *(incipient violence)* like what, am I a monster?

JERRY. I never said you // were

MARTIN. No – am I a predator? What am I? How can I make myself real to you? What must I do? *What?*

(**JERRY** *starts to exit,* **MARTIN** *pulls him back.)*

JERRY. I'm //

MARTIN. *(raging, but profoundly helpless)* Or – WHERE ARE YOU GOING – or – NO maybe I'm something you *whipped* out of the air Jerry like s-s-some pinwheel at a carnival – Right?

JERRY. (no of course // not)

MARTIN. A MONSTER? a MONSTER Jerry Is that what you want me to be?

(He grabs **JERRY** *violently and shoves his hand down* **JERRY**'s *pants.* **JERRY** *tries to push him off.)*

(rabid) HERE! HERE!

(**JERRY** *finally pulls away from him. He's shivering, he's out of breath. He tucks his shirt back in, not looking at* **MARTIN**.)

JERRY *(voice up a pitch)* You have clearly ascertained // – er

MARTIN. I love you.

JERRY. *(trying to be "rational")* – certain – feelings, feelings for uh for *me* which I –

(**MARTIN** *pulls* **JERRY**'s *face to his own and kisses him violently –* **JERRY** *not yielding as easily as he did in the previous attempt. There is something irreversible in this kiss, something ominous.)*

(**JERRY** *finally gets away. He touches his mouth. There's a bit of blood.)*

(betrayed) You...hurt me...

(A beat, then as the panic increases, the pace picks up breakneck speed, gets fast and out of control over the following:)

MARTIN *(innocent)* Did you want me to hurt you?

JERRY. You have to leave here.

MARTIN. Hurt me // back then

JERRY. I can't have this in // my house – not

MARTIN. *(quick)* You WANT pain you miss // the pain

JERRY. You have to leave // here Martin you

MARTIN. In your calves? you're empty

JERRY. have to go you // have to

MARTIN *(childlike shame)* I'm sorry

JERRY *(frightened; vehement)* GO! GO Martin LEAVE! YOU HAVE // TO

MARTIN. *(hysterical, a tantrum)* I'M SORRY JERRY I'M – *(maniacally)* DON'T DO THIS TO ME *(desperate retraction)* I'm sorry I'm sorry I'm sorry // I'm

*(Loud music cuts in as the style has tilted somewhat, gets manic, compressed. Over the following, **JERRY** holds his hands over his ears; squeezes his eyes shut. **MARTIN** touches him and **JERRY** jerks his body away, tramps to the opposite side of the room, turns to confront **MARTIN** – then squeezes his eyes shut. **MARTIN** lunges for him, desperate. **JERRY** jerks his body away, covers his ears, etc., etc.)*

JERRY. LEAVE YOU HAVE TO LEAVE HERE GET *OUT GET OUT GET* //

MARTIN. YOU'RE EMPTY JERRY I KNOW YOU! *I KNOW YOU!*

JERRY. *OUT* MARTIN GET *OUT GET OUT GET OUT GET* //

(They're both screaming at the top of their lungs, at top speed, overlapping one another, complete chaos. Lights cut off.)

4.

(Sound cuts off. Lights up.)

(We are – for the first time in the play – in **JERRY** *and* **CAROL**'s *bedroom.)*

(An open suitcase on the bed, half packed.)

*(***CAROL*** in front of the "mirror" (i.e., the fourth wall) wearing a fashionable – strikingly nontraditional wedding dress. She has a somber expression. The dress doesn't quite fit, but she looks beautiful in it. She contemplatively smoothes the silk over her stomach.)*

*(***JERRY*** enters, puncturing this sort of trance she's in. He's carrying over the agitated, confused, frightened energy from the end of the last scene.)*

CAROL. You know actually there's a parity; we sort of look alike; she's a painter she went to – what's that school in Rhode Island.

*(***JERRY*** just looks at her.)*

She's marrying another painter, they both have trust funds. *(indicates the back of the dress)* See these? Chandelier pieces; Stella McCartney, they collect sweat. *(pause)* I was just seeing what I looked like in – *(pause)* Are you alright?

JERRY. Are you – //

CAROL. Excited for your trip, I'm packing your things

JERRY. Do you want to come with me.

(beat)

CAROL. To Geneva?

JERRY. Come with me.

CAROL. Don't be stupid I have work.

(pause)

JERRY. Martin's leaving.

(She turns to him.)

CAROL. How'd that happen.

JERRY. He...he wants to go.

(beat)

CAROL. I think it's a good thing.

(She turns back, continues to adjust things.)

(long pause)

JERRY. Please...uh p-please...need me.

CAROL. What.

JERRY. I'm not a threat to you. Am I. I'm nothing. Just –

CAROL. What are you talking about I know you're not a //

JERRY. I could never harm you...

(beat)

I'm nothing, I know I'm a complete nothing I know that I'm just – baby a little baby I'm // a baby

CAROL. Stop this – why are you behaving this way?

JERRY. I just want a little pat on the head, a kiss on the cheek or something, I don't know.

CAROL. Can we talk about this later.

JERRY. I know it's...hard, but...if we //

CAROL. Don't be maudlin.

[STOP]

JERRY. Things fall apart // I mean

CAROL. *(playing with her earring in the mirror)* That's a novel by Chinua Achebe //

JERRY. THAT'S NOT WHAT I'M TALKING ABOUT!

(JERRY has grabbed her arm, pulling it – it's a bit violent actually – away from her ear.)

(CAROL looks at him. Seriously, quietly.)

CAROL *(quiet but venomous)* Don't ever touch me like that.

JERRY. *(penitent)* You're my wife.

CAROL. I'm not you're wife you don't have a wife

(beat)

you have a well-stocked *liquor* cabinet. You have a *DVD* collection. You do not. Have. A wife.

JERRY. I'm right here.

(pause)

CAROL. There's a ghost in the room.

(beat)

JERRY. You think I'm a ghost?

(She looks through him. She returns to the mirror, continues to put on her earring.)

(despair) You think I'm a ghost? *(beat; then rage)* HEY / /

(He pulls her arm and swivels her toward him, violently.)

CAROL. *(breaking free of him)* WHAT DID I JUST SAY!?

(JERRY is suddenly confused and frightened – by her as well as this odd passion consuming him.)

JERRY *(somehow ashamed to say this)* I…love you.

CAROL. Well…I love / / y

JERRY. *(rage and pain mingled)* But you're just speaking words. But I'm NOT. And I need. I need you to love me back I really. Need. That Carol – I really – I just – NOW.

CAROL. I don't

JERRY. NOW. NOW.

[STOP]

(They eyeball each other for a moment – coiled tension.)

(JERRY is breathing heavily. Music underscoring.)

(In a single gesture, looking right at her, he rips his shirt open. The buttons spill onto the floor. It is sexy and torrid and felt.)

(He approaches her. He grabs her face with his hands.)

(Just when we think he's going to kiss her he drops to his knees. In a single gesture, he grabs her waist with his hands, burying his head in her stomach, planting endless, hungry, penitent kisses. This is an act of grace. **CAROL** *is taken aback by this intimacy, and by* **JERRY**'s *uncharacteristic ardor. She looks down at him; slowly, she lifts her hand to his hair.)*

(The music bumps up.)

5.

(The following day. The Thernstroms' apartment.)

(MARTIN is moving out, he's getting together a last few things.)

(He's wearing pajamas. CAROL is reading a magazine, sipping coffee. She lights a cigarette. She's wearing the wedding dress from the previous scene.

MARTIN. Where's Jerry?

CAROL. Do you have everything?

MARTIN. You look //

CAROL. It's for a client, Jerry's on his way to the airport //

MARTIN. He's //

CAROL. He has his conference.

(beat)

MARTIN *(hurt)* Today?

CAROL. He was up packing early this morning, he said to tell you good-bye.

(beat)

MARTIN *(distant)* Oh, that's right.

CAROL. Everyone's packing. Everyone's leaving, now I'm all by my lonesome. but that's all right. I have work //

MARTIN. Do you //

CAROL. a wedding in the country, a tall-grassed Valhalla, fresh-cut flowers. *(beat)* and I have to catch up on reading and things. *(pause)* Where are you going, do you have a place?

MARTIN. I'll stay at a hotel, I guess.

CAROL. Which.

MARTIN. I don't know, I'll look for something.

CAROL. You'll look for //

MARTIN. A hotel.

CAROL. Well I know a hotel, but didn't you make reservations?

MARTIN. I thought I'd just get in a cab and just eeny meeny // miney

CAROL. Do you want to call the Pierre?

MARTIN. The Pierre, no – I don't I don't think I could afford that.

CAROL. Well where are you going to stay? I really think you should call up and reserve first, the hotels will be all booked this // time of

MARTIN. I'll be fine.

(pause)

CAROL *(reining in the impulse to control)* Well you'll find something.

(pause)

(MARTIN *returns to his last-minute packing.)*

MARTIN. How do you feel?

(CAROL *looks at* **MARTIN.)**

CAROL. Is there something in particular you'd *like* me to feel?

(beat)

MARTIN. Why do you say that.

CAROL. Because you keep asking me, "How do you feel?"

(beat)

MARTIN. I'm just concerned //

CAROL. Don't be; I'm perfect.

(beat)

MARTIN *(Sympathy)* Well *(beat)* It's sad to lose a baby.

CAROL. It wasn't a baby, it's not like – there wasn't anything, really, there wasn't anything to lose just a little glob the size of a nail clipping; it's like – blowing your nose or something – it's just //

MARTIN. But //

CAROL. Whoomp (and then a little blood but not much.)

   (beat)

MARTIN *(deep sadness)* But…it could have been something.

CAROL. Yeah and a lot of things could have been a lot of things and they weren't.

   (She lights a cigarette.)

   You don't understand: I'm not sentimental. Sentimentality is noxious, do you understand that? It's a kind of poison.

   (She drags on her virginia slim, eyeing his luggage.)

   What is that, Pierre // Cardin.

MARTIN. I think:

CAROL. It's //

MARTIN. *(continuing, with some difficulty)* I don't want to undermine what you're saying //

CAROL. Uh-huh //

MARTIN. because you're so smart about this kind of thing.

CAROL. "But"

MARTIN. *(gingerly)* Don't you feel that perhaps you're not grieving because you haven't…*lost* anything.

CAROL. That's what I said.

   (beat)

MARTIN *(not cruel, honest)* No, let me rephrase this: *(beat)* You never *wanted* a baby…so if you lost a baby you never wanted in the first place, you wouldn't feel sad, you would feel: *relieved.*

CAROL. Why would I have a child I didn't want.

MARTIN. Why *would* you?

CAROL. Well I would answer you Martin but (a) you're being invasive and rude and (b) I did want the FUCKING baby so your question is *moot.*

   (beat)

MARTIN. But you didn't.

CAROL. I did want the baby.

MARTIN. No.

CAROL. Uh – *yes*, actually, I *did.*

MARTIN. No…

CAROL. *(incredulous)* Are you now *telling* me how I feel?

MARTIN. No. *You're* telling me how you feel. Only you're not *listening.*

[STOP]

CAROL. Don't be a blockhead //

MARTIN. I'm not a // *blockhead*

CAROL. Well you're being a bit of an idiot don't you think?

MARTIN. How did we get here.

CAROL. Where //

MARTIN. This – estranged –

CAROL. It's fine //

MARTIN. It isn't fine // something's

CAROL. Look:

MARTIN. come between us Carol and I // want to

CAROL. No something USED to be between us Martin *walls* I want them *back.*

(pause)

MARTIN *(Stung)* That really hurts me.

CAROL. Well…

MARTIN. That's really hurtful, sometimes you. *(beat)* Words can do violence OK? It's a kind of violence //

CAROL. Well what's a little violence between friends. *(puffs on her cigarette glibly)* Right?

[STOP]

MARTIN. *You're so stuck //*

CAROL. I'm not // STUCK.

MARTIN. Circling in this terrible orbit //

CAROL. You're angry because we're kicking you out // alright, but don't

MARTIN. I'm not angry, no, just sad.

    (CAROL laughs.)

    (not angry) Is that funny?

CAROL. No – no –

MARTIN. *(musing)* Maybe you never experience your own sadness, so you're uncomfortable with mine.

CAROL. *(a little smug)* Yes…that must be it, "Carol the unfeeling bitch."

MARTIN. You're // not

CAROL. *(barking)* RIGHT?

MARTIN. unfeeling Carol, you feel everything; but your feelings appall you so – then you pretend they don't exist. You don't *listen.*

CAROL. I do listen.

    (CAROL grabs a glass of water and takes a sip.)

MARTIN. OK if you're listening what just happened.

CAROL. What?

MARTIN. WHAT DID YOU JUST *NOT* HEAR?

CAROL. Now you're just being crypto-annoying, I'll call the doorman // to take your

MARTIN. You don't *listen* //

CAROL. I still hear the crash of cymbals ringing in my head from the Berlioz concert two nights ago (I actually have a headache so) //

    (She pops two Advil.)

MARTIN. You did it again.

CAROL. What.

MARTIN. What just happened.

CAROL. I drank a glass of water. I drink glasses of water all the time.

MARTIN. What didn't you hear?

CAROL. I'm annoyed.

MARTIN. A certain clink of metal.

CAROL. What

MARTIN. Carol…

(**CAROL** *freezes for a moment. There's something ominous to it. She looks down at her hand. Lifts it to her face. No ring.*)

CAROL. Where is it.

MARTIN. I'm trying to *help* you // OK?

CAROL. Where *is* it?

(*beat*)

MARTIN. I took it.

CAROL. Can I have my ring.

MARTIN. (*not punishing*) I don't have it.

CAROL. Where is it.

MARTIN. I threw it in the East River.

[STOP]

(**CAROL** *laughs.*)

(**MARTIN** *laughs.*)

[STOP]

CAROL. Martin, this is sincerely not funny, now come on, where's my ring.

MARTIN. I threw it away it was garbage by your own admission.

(*pause*)

(**MARTIN** *nods, sadly, almost childlike in admission.*)

[STOP]

CAROL. *YOU TOOK MY RING?*

MARTIN. Yes.

CAROL. With the garnets.

MARTIN. Look at your eyes.

CAROL. The invincible // band?

MARTIN. Your eyes are all red.

> *(beat)*

CAROL *(wounded)* You're lying.

MARTIN. It was from love.

CAROL. Martin, *why* would you // do that

MARTIN. you said "it's too heavy"
My hand, my heart, my life,

CAROL. I //

MARTIN. "I'm tired" //

CAROL. *(protesting)* I'm NOT tired.

MARTIN. *(becoming very sad as he says it)* "I'm…*sinking*"

CAROL. *(knowing he's right)* I'm…I'm not…

MARTIN. "free // me from the lie that is my life."

> *(She massages the finger that held the ring, as if it were broken.)*

CAROL. I never…said that…

MARTIN. *(closes his eyes; an incantation)* Break Carol.

> *(beat)*

CAROL. That's not going to happen.

> *(She recovers control completely – or appears to.)*

MARTIN. It already did.

> [STOP]

CAROL. We won't press charges or anything you'll // just leave

MARTIN. You just won't see it //

CAROL. And you'll never see us // again.

MARTIN. And until you do that, until you see it that's all you'll ever be //

CAROL. HEY.
THIS IS MY LIFE.

> *(beat)*

MARTIN. It's not a life it's a shell.

CAROL. *(less sure)* And this is my // house

MARTIN. You're a shell, you said so yourself.

CAROL. I never said that.

MARTIN. You're *sinking*, that's what you // *said*

CAROL. You don't just cross the threshold Martin and walk into a person's home and say, "Fine, Carol's life, I'll WRECK it."

(She feels around her ring finger again, anxiously.)

MARTIN. *(sincerely hurt)* Is that how you perceive it?

CAROL. HOW I // PERCEIVE IT?!

MARTIN. I can certainly // understand that point of view

CAROL. "HOW I" – THAT'S WHAT YOU'VE – just get out of my house, you know what //

MARTIN. And it's valid if you subscribe to a certain worldview (but my only // qualm –)

CAROL. What "worldview" SANITY it's not a fucking WORLDVIEW it's the fucking SUBSTRATE of human existence!!!! *(icy; calm)* We won't press charges or anything. You'll just leave. Yes. You'll leave and we'll never see you again. *(beat)* Do you understand? *(beat; eyeballing him)* You will Never. See us. Again.

[STOP]

MARTIN. I //

CAROL. Leave, you're upsetting me.

[STOP]

MARTIN. Something's missing //

CAROL. Leave //

MARTIN. Carol. //

CAROL. I don't want to hear anymore //

MARTIN. But you do //

CAROL. LEAVE //

MARTIN. You want to hear all of it In the best smartest truest part of you you do want to hear it //

CAROL. *(fidgeting nervously)* JUST GET OUT OF HERE!

[STOP]

"Jerry..."

MARTIN. He's not here.

(**CAROL** *opens the front door of the apartment. She holds the door open for him.*)

[STOP]

Can I just //

CAROL. GO AWAY.

MARTIN. I just feel this is unfinished.

(beat)

Remember the apricots?

CAROL. What apricots.

MARTIN. The ones I gave you, well *(beat)* I put something in them.

(pause)

CAROL. You what?

(silence)

MARTIN. I Put something. To To cause you to...

(long pause)

(tenderly) What's the saddest thing.

(**CAROL** *begins to shake uncontrollably.*)

Is it losing something? Is that the saddest thing? No.

(beat)

It's the loss of *loss.*

Right? It's not knowing you've lost anything if you haven't experienced suffering you're *cursed* do you see that?

(beat)

And I removed it *break.*

It's OK, the curse is undone.

CAROL. You're crazy.

MARTIN. I'm // *not*

CAROL. You're crazy oh my god

MARTIN. Carol //

CAROL. *Don't say my name.*

MARTIN. I //

CAROL. *(weakly, desperate)* "Jerry…"

MARTIN. Break, it's // OK

CAROL. *(sinks helplessly down to the sofa, she's not being rational)* "Jerry…help me…Jerry…"

MARTIN. *(tears; fervid)* And that's what you were saying the whole time: "help me" but no one heard your screams – but *I* heard them; and I came to free you, to liberate you from the *suffering* you didn't know was *yours (beat)* by…giving it *back* to you *(beat)* Now it's yours again.

(For the first and only time in the play – possibly for the first time in her adult life – CAROL cries, and her crying carries with it currents that eddy backward with the force of her entire history.)

(MARTIN, deeply moved, goes to her and hugs her lovingly and, oddly, protectively, as if he'd like to shield her from the pain that he's just inflicted on her.)

(swelling with compassion) You think no one will ever know how terrified you are…But I DO KNOW.

CAROL. *(very tiny)* You…*know?*

(MARTIN nods. She looks at him. As crazy as this is, something in him makes her believe that at that moment he's the only person to have ever seen her. The rage and exasperation are still there but slowly they are eclipsed by this absolutely bizarre tenderness – it's like a trance state. MARTIN holds her face with his hands. He kisses her on the lips and she lets him.)

(He kisses her again, this time it is more overtly sexual – it's not merely erotic; it is enormously complicated. CAROL's pain is channeled into abandon as the kissing

becomes increasingly heated, almost violent. **CAROL**
starts to scream.)

*(***MARTIN** *gets more passionate, more violent.)*

(He bites out her tongue.)

*(***CAROL** *is screaming and thrashing – she backs away
in shock.)*

(He realizes what he's done.)

*(Horrified and confused – he spits her tongue out of his
mouth in full view of the audience.)*

*(***CAROL** *stands there in shock – shaking uncontrollably,
making inaudible little noises.)*

*(***MARTIN** *'s breathing gets heavier.)*

MARTIN. *(to himself)* OK: what's my ethic?

(pause)

I'm in the m-m-molec…

(weakly) I'm

I'm…

(He looks down at the extirpated tongue. A pause.)

(A horrified recognition; it has gone too far.)

(He starts to retch.)

Oh god.

(He covers his mouth.)

(stops himself)

(slowly raises his gaze to meet **CAROL***)*

No

(He can't look.)

No no no no no.

*(He squeezes his eyes shut, shakes his head wildly,
wishing it away.)*

MARTIN. HELP. HELP ME.

    [STOP]

    (grasping at straws) No it can't be wrong – It's –

    (He shuts his eyes, tries to concentrate.)

    (Opens his eyes. Nods sadly, like a small boy.)

    (He grabs a sharp knife from the kitchen.)

    (He goes to the chopping block.)

    *(**CAROL** sees him and starts screaming.)*

    (He cuts off his finger, weeping from pain. He holds up his severed hand, the blood pulsing out. A nightmare.)

    (A crack of thunder; the rain beats down.)

    *(**MARTIN** is still holding the knife.)*

    *(**CAROL** backs up, afraid for her life.)*

    *(**CAROL** runs to the door, runs out of the apartment.)*

MARTIN. WAIT –

    *(**MARTIN** runs after her, leaving the door open.)*

    (long silence)

    *(**JERRY** enters with luggage. He's holding the mail in his hand. He's sopping wet from the rain. He hangs up his coat in the closet.)*

JERRY *(calls out)* Darling, the new issue of *Harper's*! Carol, the flight was canceled, the weather is…

    (He mumbles the rest.)

    (As he walks to the sofa, he slides on the waxed floors.)

    (oh these damn…)
Carol??

    (He sits on the sofa and opens the magazine.)

    (He checks his watch. The storm outside is raging.)

Carol??

(He removes his jacket. Folds it neatly over the sofa. He sits back comfortably on the sofa. He starts to put his feet up, then just as they are about to land on the naked, sparkling clean table he remembers to take his shoes off, which he does, with élan – pleased that he remembered the house rule. Puts them on the shoe rack. He goes to the bar and is about to pour himself a drink. Just as he's about to pour – he stops himself. He considers for a moment. He puts down the liquor. He puts the glass back. He sighs. Moves back to the sofa, sits. He puts on his glasses and reads the cover of the magazine.)

(reading aloud) Salman Rushdie declares jihad on HarperCollins...

(He's intrigued. He flips a page of the magazine gaily.)

(sings, smiling as he reads:)

"You made me love you
I didn't want to do it
I di –"

(A sharp crack of thunder cuts him off.)

(Blackout.)

End of Act Two

ACT THREE

1.

[TITLE: "Breaking Up"]

(A thunderclap – and the lights snap on. **JUDY** and **JERRY** in **JERRY**'s apartment.)

(A few hours after the end of Act Two. It's still raining.)

(**JUDY**'s hair – replete with the white shock from Act Two – is now a frizzed mess, echoing, but not too overtly, Elsa Lanchester in The Bride of Frankenstein. She's wearing her best outfit – possibly a Chanel suit, but dusted with spots of ash and someburnt patches. She's clearly been in a fire. She's got a scrapbook with her. She seems – oddly – more lucid than we've ever seen her. Which is not to say she's entirely lucid – she's in the throes of deep inner conflict.)

(**JERRY** looks as he did at the end of Act Two. He's got a bit of a stutter now. There's a box of empty liquor bottles by his side, and on the coffee table are a cheese board, a few used plates, some silverware, a box of marrons glacés.)

(The colors, clothing, etc., should be conspicuously muted here – no more bright colors, patterns. The pace is different here, too – it's more awkward, slower, more haphazard, more fraught. There's white noise in the silences, it's sort of viscid, thick.)

JERRY. And you say you just *couldn't* find an electrician.

(**JUDY** shrugs, gestures with her hands.)

(doesn't know how to react – mainly to her hair) Judy uh uh
– I mean – th-this is *terrible,* where are you going to *go?*

JUDY. Well; I mean – I came here.

JERRY. D-do you have any…money?

JUDY. I have a little in a bank account.

JERRY. Well – that's h-h-heartening.

JUDY. I have a trust fund. My mother controls it. *(beat)* I
could stay with my mother. *(beat)* Though to be honest
with you I hate my mother; she hates me too – we're
very…*symbiotic* – in our hate. *(beat)* I'll probably have a
conversation with her about it at some point.

JERRY. That's – a shame.

JUDY. No, I've learned to embrace it.

(JERRY nods encouragingly. Pause.)

(JUDY leafs through her scrapbook.)

JERRY. Well…you're – always welcome here you know.

JUDY. Am I?

JERRY. Of course darling, of *c-course* you are.

(beat)

JUDY. I have to say: I…*demurred* – when I considered
coming here Jerry. Because – isn't Martin staying here?

JERRY. M-m-n-
No – NO – no no – he h-h-h

JUDY. *(with purpose)* Is he here? Because that would be
awkward. Do you know he never insured the house?
so now I don't have a place to live. It's. *(Getting caught
up in the sadness. Beat)* But that's how women in third-
world countries live all the time;

JERRY. That's true Judy.

(beat)

JUDY. especially victims of genocide.

(beat)

JERRY. Well – // actually I think

JUDY. *Is* Martin here? It's alright, you can speak openly with me, I'm a realist now.

JERRY. M-m-m- he's – uh – you know g-g

JUDY. *(kind of annoyed)* Jerry you're stuttering.

JERRY. N-n-not so mm-m

JUDY. I can't understand you.

JERRY. Martin's g-g-g – he m-moved *out.*

JUDY. Why are you speaking this way?

JERRY. Oh. Well – I mean it could be – Judy I've quit drinking! I nearly forgot all about it. I spilled it all down the drain – th-th-they say you experience withdrawal but I'm – I-I-I'm I mean look at me –

(He holds out his hand, it's shaking wildly.)

(surprised) Oh.

(He watches his hand shake. She does too.)

Well – it's not TOO bad is it?

(It shakes some more.)

JUDY. Jerry, may I be frank?

(pause)

Your – alcoholism has been an incredibly...destructive force; not only in my life, but in the lives of other people.

(He looks at her. She seems to be **JUDY,** *but is she?)*

JERRY. Alcoholic? I – I wouldn't call myself that.

*(***JUDY** *sighs.)*

I – maybe drank a l-l-little bit more than I // should maybe

JUDY. NO you're actually an *alcoholic. Jerry.* And it's been taxing on everyone. *(beat)* You always gave everything this sheen of fun? but there wasn't any fun. You demanded all the attention and then sucked the energy out of the room when you had it. it wasn't fun. You were incoherent – and I exerted a lot of effort

in pretending to understand what you were saying –
when you actually weren't making any sense! *That's not
my fucking JOB Jerry!*

(*pause*)

I mean I. like you Jerry. I'm. Just trying to be clear about
how your choices impact the lives of other people.

[STOP]

JERRY. I think this is – *tremendously* – exciting, Judy...

(*She looks at him – surprised by his reaction.*)

you're exhibiting a – real – *intrapsychic* – *wellness*...it's
really v-vvery heartening – truly.

(*pause*)

JUDY (*Now oddly fragile*) Thanks for being so nice.

(*Now that she's won she's plagued with guilt.*)

Because it's hard for me to articulate. You know to say
what I. To say what...

(*She tries to undo the crying but can't.* **JERRY** *pats her
knee avuncularly, looks at her sweetly. He offers her a
marron glacé – she doesn't notice. He eats it himself.*)

Sometimes it comes out this way.
I'm actually very strong.

(*pause*)

I know how to fix it I think.
I'm much more lucid than I seem.

(**JERRY** *nods, an analyst now. A contemplative pause.*)

JERRY. Do you want to put on some m-*makeup*? Or.

JUDY. Because I thought about it and I realized, "Well Judy,
at least you're not a *torture* victim, you're just divorced!"
(*She laughs, a little too loud.*) I'm in a good mood now,
aren't you? I love the sound of the rain, I wish it would
rain forever!

(**JERRY** *smiles, a bit strained.*)

JERRY. What's that book you're holding?

JUDY. A scrapbook!

JERRY. It's nice to k-k-keep scrapbooks Judy.

JUDY. It's been healing. Do you really see an intrapsychic wellness in me?

JERRY. You seem just m-marvelous Judy – you've really rebounded – do you want s-s-some lipstick or something Carol must have some // lying ar –

JUDY. No I don't like lipstick anymore. I don't see why women should have to disguise their faces for men. Men should be attracted to my face as it is. This is my face, and if men don't like it they can go *fucking rip out their eyeballs.*

(**JERRY** *freezes, smiles a sickly smile.*)

(barely holding back tears) I'm sorry if I'm being inappropriate – but it's important to say what one feels. I think I'm becoming a whole person now.

JERRY. Well that's the important thing Judy, wholeness, I mean, it's just t-t-terribly important to be whole, and to find things that fulfill you at that deep errrrrrr You know level. It's just m-m-marvelous.

(long pause)

JUDY. So are you excited Jerry?

(He smiles.)

JERRY. Ex*ci*ted?

(He looks at her.)

JUDY. About the *baby*!

[STOP]

(He freezes; the smile freezes, starts to crack.)

JERRY *(not getting up)* L-l-let me get you a drink // Judy.

JUDY. Oh, I'm not thirsty

JERRY. Are you s-s-sure?

JUDY. What's the matter? *(pause)* Jerry?

(JERRY smiles, shrugs. An awkward moment. He starts to – nervously – pick out his eyebrow hairs.)

JERRY *(seeing her face)* What. Oh *these*. Oh HA HA: oh they just fall out! *Face* it Judy we're getting older: things fall out! A ha ha.

(He absentmindedly sprinkles the extirpated eyebrow hairs onto the floor, the sofa; then, instantly, realizes he's done this and – worried about the mess – tries to recover them.)

What about a snack – a little snack, perhaps a *marron glacé?* – You see Judy, they wrap them in these pretty gold papers I like that. (Don't you think that's *classy* Judy, *gold* –) Oh you have to try this…oh I think I'll have JUST one more, I don't – *(He stops. Looks over to her. A beat)* What's the matter, darling?

(He opens a marron glacé as he speaks – rather rapidly, lots of nervous energy.)

(JUDY spots CAROL's tongue lying fugitive on the floor. JUDY moves closer, scrunching up her face, trying to make out what it is.)

What do you have there darling?

(JUDY examines it a moment before responding.)

JUDY. Is…that a *tongue?*

JERRY. *(curious, furrowed brow)* Tongue?

(JERRY picks up the tongue with a fork.)

(JERRY puts on his glasses and examines it. He puts it on a plate and wiggles it around.)

(He sniffs it.)

(A beat.)

(He turns to JUDY.)

Gosh. That's – kind of *weird*. Do you think it's a *human* tongue?

JUDY. What else could it be Jerry?

(They stare at it.)

JERRY. It could be, well…who knows – a – *cat* tongue.

JUDY. Cat?

(beat)

JERRY. Err *(making it up as he goes)* cats always, well they –
like to – c-c-c-creep around. Into. Those – pneumatic
– *pipes* and things, right? maybe – uh. Who *knows* it…
sort of creeped around uh into one of our pipes and –
had an accident!

JUDY. Yeah I don't know.

JERRY. It's possible anything's POSSible – cats – *slink*
around have you ever seen a cat – Judy – like this have
you ever *(He does an imitation of a cat "slinking".)* and
then they sort of – *(more slinking)* they SLINK – they – I
mean am I RIGHT?! – HAHAHA – they – th-th-th-th
aha ha ha…

*(MARTIN has entered the room – he is wearing nothing
but his pajamas, now soaked. He's been standing there
unseen, shell-shocked into silence, watching them.)*

Well anyway *(excited)* HEY: are you hungry? because we
have some of this marvelous quince paste and some of
this really // just excellent Man*che*go artisanal –

JUDY. I'm really // not very

JERRY. from – *Oh* and we have these new knives we just
sharpened we have a nice runny *l'Edel de Cleron*! Oh
and the rind is *edible* too now how's //

MARTIN. *(blurt; a child)* I hurt Carol.

(JERRY freezes.)

JERRY *(to JUDY)* What's that, dear?

JUDY. I didn't…say anything.

[STOP]

*(JERRY furrows his brow, considers. He shrugs and
returns to the cheese.)*

JERRY. You know Judy: *cheese* is the *corpse* of *milk* – did you
know that? there's – a Dutch biologist wrote a // whole

JUDY. I said I didn't want cheese.

JERRY. Well that's f-fine Judy, no one has to eat anything
they don't want to eat, that's a h-h-hallmark of civilized
society.

(beat)

MARTIN. I – *hurt* Carol.

*(**JERRY** stops. He looks left, then right.)*

*(He turns, sees **MARTIN**. Stands.)*

JERRY. Uh.

*(**JUDY** sees him now. Her posture changes, stiffens, her
comportment.)*

(They look at each other.)

(silence)

JUDY. Hello.

(pause)

JERRY. I – I – err. You haven't…*gone?* I…uh…

*(**MARTIN** cannot make eye contact with him.)*

MARTIN. She died.

(pause)

It was like an orchid The way her her dress spread In
the river

(pause)

She just kept…*sinking.* I went in to get her but.

(pause)

I tried to…

(They look at him – utter stupefaction.)

[STOP]

(**JERRY** *eats marrons glacés, and cheese, and anything he sees, and he smiles, and he nods approvingly.* **MARTIN** *just looks on at them. This goes on for a while.*)

Carol // is

JERRY. Carol is d-dead Yes I heard. It's f-f-fine. It's perfectly *fine* Martin.

(**JERRY** *eats, hums.*)

(*mouthful of food*) My god this Manchego is scrumptious – oh Judy you must try this it's so earthy! Just dd-delicious!

(*He stuffs his face. Smiles contentedly. Blocks it all out.*)

(*He looks down at the tongue.*)

(*beat*)

(*smile falls*)

(*beat*)

(*chewing stops*)

(*short pause*)

(*starts to retch – spits out the food on his plate*)

(*pause*)

(*looks around at them – smiles a strained smile*)

R-raw milk cheeses a ha ha…You know h-how it

[STOP]

I must clear off to bed: I'm *terribly* s-sleepy.

MARTIN. I learnt it wrong.

(*pause*)

(*can't look at him*) I'm sorry.

JERRY. *Learn*? *"learn"*? I don't kn-kn-kn –

[STOP]

(*as if this was a clever joke he didn't quite get*) Ha ha ha ha – oh. (*He sighs.*) You can make your b-b-bed Judy can't you the // sheets are in the

MARTIN. I couldn't…I – tried to //

JERRY. *(obscenely casual)* Whatever you want to do is all right with me. *We do our best.*

JUDY. Jerry has promised me the sofa so I don't know if. It's *possible* but we would have to – forge – boundaries, certain – You really – should leave but the weather is so bad I don't – want you to catch cold. You look cold. You. *(She looks at him.)* I don't want you to be…*sick* – I'll…change your pajamas.

JERRY. Good night.

*(**JERRY** starts to exit for the bedroom.)*

JUDY. Jerry he – he needs to – change into –

*(**MARTIN** looks at her. Touches her face very sweetly, very sadly. She melts. She clasps his hand. He looks into her eyes very tenderly.)*

(silence)

MARTIN. *We're dying.*

[STOP]

*(**MARTIN** stands; looks down at the knife a few beats. Grabs the knife, cuts his own neck.)*

(Lights shift. Time starts to warp, slow down.)

*(A scream comes, faraway, hollow, distant. **JERRY** looks away. **MARTIN** holds his throat, drops the knife, collapses in slow motion.)*

*(**JUDY**'s face contorts into a frozen scream.)*

(The sound of screaming enters her throat like a blast of wind.)

(The world breaks open.)

2.

(The scream gets louder, higher, reduplicates, multiple tracks, pitches, timbres. A propulsive, savage machinery.)

(The sound gets louder and louder then abruptly cuts off.)

(After a few beats, we hear the droney sounds of a video game – pong?)

*(A few beats. Then the tiny glow from a game boy that **JERRY**'s playing.)*

*(A faint glow on **JERRY**. His denial has compounded. He's lost in the game, giddy, quietly laughing to himself.)*

*(**JUDY** enters with lit candles, places them throughout the room.)*

*(We see that **MARTIN**'s body is sprawled on the sofa.)*

(The rain and thunder are worse than ever – it's really coming down.)

*(**JERRY**'s body is shaking somewhat from the DTs. His stutter is worse.)*

JUDY. Where are they?

JERRY. (Oh I'll g-get you I'll – get you I'll –)

JUDY. Jerry stop playing that. *(pause; she grabs it violently from him)* STOP IT

JERRY. Oh – now you made me l-l-l-lose – you made me lose the whole – *(weird spin into violence)* GAME. GOD FFUCKING DAMNIT!

(long pause)

*(**JUDY** goes to **MARTIN**'s corpse, feels his wrist – futilely – for a pulse.)*

JUDY. Where's the ambulance, it's been nearly an hour.

*(**JERRY** looks over at her.)*

The power's not //

[STOP]

I don't – *feel* right.

(*pause*)

(JUDY *looks around at the fractured landscape that was once a living room. It's terrifying.*)

Where…*are* we.

(JERRY *is clearly panicking, but tries to hide it. He looks around a bit.*)

JERRY. Well – errr – we're in m-m-my h-house…this is my – err – living room – th-th-there's just a bit of a blackout – but – it'll all be…it'll b-b-be just – just – j-j-just…er…

(*As* JERRY *is speaking* JUDY *has made her way to the window. Looks out. Freezes – it's ominous.* JERRY *sees her – stops speaking. Everything goes silent except for the sound of the rain.*)

(*terrified*) Judy?

(*silence*)

(*tears*) It's…all…*flooded* //

(JERRY *slowly, tentatively, makes his way to the widow. He looks out.*)

What are those…*floaty* things?

(JUDY *can't speak to respond.* JERRY *suddenly realizes they're bodies. Panic.*)

Oh. oh – uh –

(*He turns away.*)

JUDY. (*terrified*) Jerry – please – I don't know what to do, can you – help // me I

JERRY. OK OK – uh – let me th-think –
Judy
"I…*believe*."

(*She stops. She remembers.*)

(She turns, slowly, to him −)

(a tiny smile)

JUDY. Tinkerbell?

(She looks at him.)

(She nods. She's a girl again, just for a flash.)

(She laughs − but too much...he laughs too without knowing why.)

(It stops.)

(A pause.)

(Back to the impossible reality.)

(She looks away for a moment.)

(She turns to JERRY. *Something in her has died now.)*

(She looks at him for a moment.)

(She kisses him on the forehead.)

(She crosses right in front of him, takes the knife off the table. Looks at it.)

(A beat.)

JERRY. *(gingerly, frightened)* Wh-wh-where are you going?

(pause)

JUDY. *(very sweetly)* Play your game.

JERRY. B-b-b-

JUDY. *(sad for him)* I'll be...right back.

(He looks to her, very afraid. He knows. She walks quietly in the bedroom − shuts the door behind her. He watches, helpless.)

[STOP]

(He retrieves his game. Tries to play. It's dead.)

JERRY. HEY − the battery w-w-w-

The – oh – FUCK
FUCK
FUCK.

(*pause*)

(*a frightened whisper*) Judy?

(*He looks to the bedroom – he's thinking of going in but can't bring himself to see what's happened.*)

(**JUDY** *come quick.*)

(*pause*)

Carol….are you in there?

(*fillip of panic*)

Judy stop tr-tr-tricking me it's not f-f-funny.

(*He goes to* **MARTIN**.)

This isn't funny old man now g-g-get up. come on – let's get you a nice bath Where's the gin.

(*silence*)

WHERE'S MY GIN.

(*pause*)

OK.
Oh.
Oh I see.

(**JERRY** *laughs to himself, it's a bit nuts.*)

(*He plunks down next to* **MARTIN**'s *corpse; turns to* **MARTIN**.)

Well! (*He looks at him.*) This is a ch-challenge.

(*He laughs – but it's despairing. His body is shaking from the DTs.*)

[STOP]

(*He sees a Bible.*)

(*stops laughing*)

(Looks at **MARTIN**. *Looks at Bible.)*

(Gathers more energy around this.)

(to himself) you can undo it.

(He slowly picks up the Bible. Clasps it to him.)

Y-y you can –

YES YOU F-F-F-F-Fucking can.

You inflict the wound, you can't lance it *I* have to do that.

(beat; increasingly fervid; he opens the Bible, eyes gleaming.)

I HAVE TO DO IT. I HAVE TO DO IT.

(He's shaking crazily, turning pages, frenetically, clumsily. He looks at **MARTIN**. *Stands. Puts on his glasses, hands trembling. Reads from Corinthians 15:52. He starts slowly, tentatively. It builds into evangelical zeal.)*

W-w-w-we shall not all s-sleep,

but we shall all be ch-changed.

In a moment…

In the twinkling of an eye…

at the l-last trump. for the tr-trumpet shall sound…

and the dead…

shall be r-r-r-aised

inc-corruptible.

and we shall be…*ch-changed.*

(He looks at **MARTIN**. *He waits.)*

(He looks at **MARTIN**.*)*

Nothing. Nothing.

(He looks away – starts to weep: he's totally lost now.)

(The lights change.)

(Suddenly – almost imperceptibly – a hand moves.)

*(The hand lifts. We see it but **JERRY** does not.)*

*(**MARTIN** 's eyes open.)*

MARTIN. Jerry?

*(**JERRY** opens his eyes.)*

Hi…

*(He slowly, cautiously turns to **MARTIN**.)*

JERRY. M-m-m-m-

Martin *(playfully)* Hiiii Jerrry…

*(**JERRY** covers his mouth with his hand and shakes; he's totally flustered, complete disbelief.)*

JERRY. M-M-M-M-

MARTIN. It's *me*.

Jerry it's me.

*(**MARTIN** sits upright – turns to **JERRY**.)*

(He feels his face, chest: blood; laughs.)

Oh; gee – I'm bleeding – don't worry I feel fine.

JERRY. M-m-m-m-m-m-m-

MARTIN. You're shaking.

JERRY. I I I I –

MARTIN. Scared?

*(**JERRY** nods yes, like a child. He starts to weep – a deep release.)*

Sshhhhh. it's OK, look, I'm here:

*(**JERRY** nods no – he has a terribly worried expression – trauma.)*

Don't be afraid: it *worked*: *look* – it all worked out, just as you said.

(beat)

You were *right*…

People *are* disconnected from their lives…

*(**JERRY** looks at him.)*

but You're a *whole person* now…

JERRY. I'm I'm –

MARTIN. The *fundaments*…right?

    (**JERRY** *looks at him – nods yes.*)

JERRY. You're my f-friend…

MARTIN. *Right* Jerry?

JERRY. *Kn-know* each other

MARTIN. Want me to hold you?

JERRY. B-baby…

    (**JERRY** *– still tremoring wildly – nods yes frenetically.*)

MARTIN. Yes, you're just a little baby aren't you?

    (**JERRY** *laughs, he weeps in* **MARTIN***'s arms.*)

    (**JUDY** *enters wearing the wedding dress. Her hair is beautiful, the shock of white is gone. She is the Ideal* **JUDY***.*)

    (*She sees* **MARTIN**. **JERRY** *looks up.*)

JUDY. Martin?

    (**MARTIN** *looks at her, smiles.* **JERRY** *is panicked all over again, turning to* **JUDY**, *then back to* **MARTIN**, *again and again, both frightened and amazed.*)

JERRY *(to* **JUDY***)* Y-y-y-you –   *(looks to* **MARTIN**, *then back)* He c-c-came back he c-c-c –

JUDY. *(incredulous)* Martin?

    (**JUDY** *smiles. She laughs joyfully. They all laugh.*)

    (*This all has the tenor of a dream.*)

    (*The wind gets louder outside. The storm gets more intense.*)

    (*The walls start to shake.*)

    (**JUDY** *looks around – frightened.*)

    (*The door to the apartment blows open.*)

    (**CAROL** *is standing at the threshold.*)

(She stands there for a moment. Then enters – dripping wet. She is something dredged up from Atlantis.)

(But something is different about her, aside from her appearance, and slowly we realize what it is: she has developed the tragic, shattered nobility of someone who's been stripped of all vestments of civilization.)

*(****JERRY*** *is shaking with tears.)*

JERRY. C-c-Carol…I was right – I was *right*: we fall and rise and are *risen* l-l-like empires – Torn asunder, made one f-flesh…b-broken, repaired. This is g-g-g-God's grace, it is – I see it now.

(He shakes and tremors wildly.)

I-I s-see it…

*(Slowly, shakily, weakly and with some effort, **CAROL** lifts her left hand, her fingers slightly spread.)*

CAROL. I'm Not Broken.

*(On her finger is the ring **MARTIN** deposited in the East River: miraculously retrieved.)*

(The ring gleams.)

*(As the lights begin to fade, **CAROL**'s patina of strength, as it were, quickly starts to erode. Her lips quaver, the tears well in her eyes. There's a deep, disconsolate sadness in her.)*

*(****JERRY*** *closes his eyes, smiling slightly, moving his lips; a garbled, fevered prayer. Tableau.)*

End of Play